THE
MACARONI
CHRISTMAS
Tree

THE
MACARONI
CHRISTMAS
Tree

A novel by

Marilyn Brown

SALT
PRESS

Springville, Utah

ISBN: 1-55517-581-3
v.1

Published by Salt Press
Cedar Fort Inc.
www.cedarfort.com

Distributed by:

Typeset by Kristin Nelson
Cover design by Adam Ford
Cover design © 2001 by Lyle Mortimer
Illustrations by Simeen Brown

Printed in the United States of America
10 9 8 7 6 5 4 3 2 1

Printed on acid-free paper

r

For Jordan Flake

. . . who valiantly wrote a winning essay
to help preserve Academy Square.

1

It was a good thing there weren't very many people in the Christmas tree lot. Elaine was squealing and Sylvia was running up and down the rows of trees pointing to the big ones, yelling, "This one, this one," at the top of her two-year-old lungs.

We were stopping often, looking at the big spruce trees as if we could afford two or three of them. The plump needles smelled as piney as if they had just been cut—although we knew they had been in the lot for a long time. It was close to Christmas. We had been waiting for Papa to come to Provo from Bremerton, Washington, and when he arrived, the first thing he did was take us to Mr. Sundbloom's store with the string of Christmas lights on the fence around his parking lot, the fresh-smelling trees standing in clumps under the night sky.

The other people in the lot tried to ignore us, though it must have been hard. Mother herded us toward the back of the lot near the store so that we would be out of sight. Elaine began puffing white clouds of breath and whistling like a steam engine. I complained to Mother, asking her to stop Elaine, for she was embarrassing us, but Mother brought it to my attention that it was important for Elaine to breathe—that everyone else in the lot was blowing white breath. I was just beginning to protest when Mr. Sundbloom came up to us from behind the big lighted window in the market where he had been sitting with his pipe in his mouth, the smoke encircling his head like a wreath—a revised version of Santa Claus from the Christmas poem. Since we looked like the largest, most threatening family in the tree lot, he stopped us and said, "You the McKinseys?"

My pa looked up. He didn't know Mr. Sundbloom then, because my pa had not been living with us. He had been in Bremerton, Washington, where he was finishing up with World War II while Mom and we three girls (I was the oldest) had come the year before to the middle of the country to find safety. We felt very fortunate to have him home for a few days for Christmas, and he was determined to follow our tradition of getting a nice Christmas tree—even though this year we were still living in a tiny yellow stucco house next to the M&M grocery store. If we couldn't have a large house, at least we could have a beautiful tree—at least as beautiful as we would have had in Bremerton, if we had still been there and taken our annual trip out onto the hillside to cut our own.

I remembered cutting our own tree as though it were yesterday, my father with his ax in hand and the baby Sylvia in a sling. When I got tired of climbing the mountain, I had grabbed onto the back of Papa's belt with both hands and his pants fell down! That was Christmas in Washington. Now we were in Podunk, Utah, in the Christmas tree lot, and suddenly Mr. Sundbloom, with the pipe in his mouth, was asking between his teeth, "Are you the McKinseys?"

He should have known, because several times he had seen my mom come into his store that sat at the back of the Christmas tree lot on Third South. I realized, however, that he probably never knew her name until now.

"That's us," my pa said.

"My wife says you got a call on my telephone inside the store. It beats all hellfire how they found you."

As soon as Mr. Sundbloom said "hellfire," my ma's face went white. It was true that if she'd had time she would have covered up the ears of every one of us girls to protect us from such strong language, but that wasn't the full reason she caught her breath. It was because earlier in the evening she had heard that my papa's aunt, Selby Blue, who lived in the old McKinsey mansion up on Fifth West, was getting along poorly, and earlier that afternoon Ma had told the neighbor lady that if Selby wanted us, to call Sundbloom's where we would be looking for a Christmas tree.

"It's Selby Blue," my father guessed at once. "I'm afraid it's Selby Blue."

"Well, all right," Mother said. "If she needs us, tell her we'll come immediately."

My father lumbered toward the big store at the back of the lot to answer the phone, and for a few minutes we waited in the cut forest blowing steamy clouds with our breath. When he returned, he nodded his head to say yes, it was Selby Blue.

We hadn't had time to get a tree. When we climbed back into the Chevrolet, I hung on the window and watched the forest of plump blue-needled trees grow smaller and smaller behind us as though they were backing away from us waving their feathery arms. Finally every one of them faded to the size of pin heads and vanished away.

2

It was indeed Selby Blue's neighbor, Mrs. Oscar, who had talked on the telephone to Pa. Selby had said she would like to see her nephew Bill McKinsey immediately.

This wasn't the first time we had dropped something important to see Aunt Selby. Selby Blue Raine had been fighting a cold—and maybe pneumonia—for several weeks now, though she refused to go to the hospital. She had always insisted that the minute she was gone, her oldest sister, Virginia Stockton, would bring her dogs and cats and furniture from Fort Collins and move in.

On the way to the mansion, my father explained that Aunt Virginia was the oldest in the family. Virginia believed that she, instead of Selby Blue, should have owned the mansion when their father died. One of Virginia's sons, Chandler Stockton, was a real estate broker in Salt Lake City, and Papa thought this son and his wife Evelyn were itching to get hold of the old mansion and sell it for a lot of money.

When we drove down Center Street past the bright windows, we asked all kinds of questions: "What's going to happen if Aunt Selby Blue dies?" We knew Selby Blue's husband died many years ago, and her only son was killed in the war. She didn't have an heir. "Will Virginia's son come by and just take the house and all of Aunt Selby Blue's rugs and furniture and sell them, too?" When it seemed the answer wasn't coming, Elaine piped up, "Can we buy some?"

"Aunt Selby Blue is only eighty years old. She still has lots of years left," my pa said. Of course, he thought Aunt Selby should last as long as Grandfather Bale Matthew McKinsey, who built the house with money he made investing in the railroads, and had just turned ninety-eight when he died.

"Can we go in to see her?" Elaine asked.

"If you promise to be quiet," Pa said.

When we drove north on Fifth West, we gazed with awe at the entire row of very nice big houses on the east side of the street. Some were sparkling with Christmas lights hooked inside the windows. The McKinsey mansion, with its big yard on the south, was the nicest house on the block, but there were no lights in it. It was as dark as a tomb.

When Papa stopped the car, Elaine kicked open the car door. Noisily, she jumped out onto the sidewalk and began running for no reason—waving her six-year-old arms. Up and down the narrow sidewalk, she ran—back and forth, back and forth in the gray light from the street lamp only a half block away. Then she ran back and forth in front of the other houses on the block where the Christmas lights were still burning.

Baby Sylvia stood on the car seat by Mother, and sucked her thumb. Father and Mother and I sat still looking at the dark house. "You could have asked Mrs. Oscar to leave the lights on for us," Mother said.

"It's after nine. Aunt Selby probably went to bed. And lately she hasn't been able to afford much electricity," Father said. "I told Mrs. Oscar I'd be right over. She must have thought we would know how to turn on the lights."

I sat on the back seat, watching Elaine pump her arms up and down while she rushed crazily about on the sidewalk just because she was excited about being at the old mansion. I always thought it looked like there were ghosts in it. But Elaine acted like she was about to see Santa Claus.

Papa continued, "We have to remember that Aunt Selby is probably in bed. She needs lots of rest. Aunt Virginia and her son and his wife Evelyn from Salt Lake City have been in charge lately. Selby told me that she is most concerned about Virginia taking over the house. What she would really like is for our family to live in it."

Mother gasped and put her hand on her chest, as though the prospect of inheriting the McKinsey mansion was both exciting and overwhelming.

"Let's just be quiet going in," Papa said.

3

When Papa knocked on the door, Mother put Sylvia down on the porch, but Sylvia burst into a scream that would have frightened all of the ghosts of the McKinsey mansion into a catatonic condition. So Mother picked her up in her arms again.

With that kind of noisy warning, it was naturally not very long before Mrs. Oscar came out. "Oh, she will be so glad to see you. I'm sorry it's so dark. She doesn't want any lights shining."

By now our eyes were getting used to it. There was enough light from the street that we could see the mansion. With heavy walls of sturdy red brick, it looked as though it were built to last six hundred years. There were the first and second floors, and then an attic and a basement. Mother said there were four stories. I had never known what *stories* were until we came to Provo and visited Aunt Selby Blue. At first I thought Mother meant there were four separate books written about the house, but I soon learned it meant *floors*. I thought that could have meant story books as well, one very different one for each floor. There should have been at least three books written about the house.

After Selby Blue had inherited the place from my father's grandfather Bale Matthew McKinsey, she proceeded to live in it for sixty years. Bale had trusted her, my father said. She was to keep the house intact forever, which he believed would have been difficult for the oldest child in the family, Virginia—who had a penchant for dividing and conquering everything.

As it was, Selby Blue was married to her husband Mort Raine for only five years. He died suddenly of an aneurism at thirty-six, lifting one too many cartons of cottage cheese out of the dairy wagon. Selby was further devastated when their only son, Beauregard, was killed in the war fifteen years later. She had kept herself glued to the house as though it had taken the place of her family. Virginia Stockton, who always believed the house should have been hers, could never have lived there anyway, because her husband, Chandler Stockton, took a job with the Budweiser Brewery and they had found themselves living in Fort Collins, Colorado.

In the front of the house were five steps that led up to a thick square-pillared porch about the size of a small room. A brick wall surrounded the porch. Above the porch were two bedroom windows like huge observant eyes, the one on the left a bay window, larger than the other. As I got used to the dark, I could see beyond the big wood door and the heavy leaded glass. We had been in the front room several times, but never in the back bedroom. With few lights in the house, we had to grope our way along the corridor until my father found a light switch, and even then, the bulb must have been only twenty watts, it was so dim.

As Mrs. Oscar took us into the back bedroom, we gazed in awe. It was a huge room with high ceilings and thick red brocade drapes hung with broad rows of gold tassels flecked with silver. Shiny pieces of old furniture with carved legs of polished walnut stood like old guardians, waiting and watching to see what was going to happen to their friend Selby Blue. A bookcase in the corner with doors of leaded glass held old leather volumes and a set of some old encyclopedias. In the center of the room at the far wall was the huge bed. And in the middle of the bed lying in a pool of faded light was little Selby Blue. Her hair was so gray it looked blue. Her head looked small, like a cabbage. She turned toward us as we came in, and smiled.

4

"Oh, Bill, I'm so glad you're here," Aunt Selby said in a thin voice resembling the squeak in our washing machine. "Did you get a Christmas tree?" She seemed a little worried. "I'm allergic to pine needles."

"No," Papa said. "That's not the important thing. You mustn't worry about it. We're here for you."

"I'm pretty sure I have a non-allergenic Christmas tree I made still somewhere in this house."

"Please don't worry. The important thing is that we need to get you well."

"I have some popsicle sticks," she said. "I can make a Christmas tree out of popsicle sticks. The children should have a Christmas tree." She was trying to raise her head up off the pillow. "At any rate, we'll have Christmas here. I am not going to the hospital."

My father acknowledged Mrs. Oscar, who just rolled her eyes. He bent over his old aunt and put his hand on her brow. "Aunt Selby, if you're not feeling good, are you sure that's not where you ought to go?"

"I'm sure," she said. "They'll just put tubes in me, and I don't want tubes in me." She had enough fight left to frown. "This is where Mort will look for me."

Mort Raine had been dead for fifty-four years. Elaine said to Mother, "I don't think he would remember after fifty-four years, would he?"

Mother hushed her, patting her back. "Shhh. Of course. He'd always remember. But we don't know. Let Papa take care of it," she said.

"Mrs. Oscar can't always be here to fill all of your needs. Do you want me to hire some special nurses?"

Aunt Selby Blue turned her head toward the red brocade gold-tasseled drapes on the window. "No," she said. "Bring me the popsicle sticks. They are in the bottom drawer of the chifforobe."

My mother began to open the drawer while Selby turned to Papa. "I'm so sorry to interrupt your Christmas, Bill. And to be allergic to Christmas trees. But I need you. Can't you bring your family to the house and live here? You can stay here for as long as you need to stay here. You can have the house if you want it." And then in words barely audible to the human ear, she added, "So Virginia won't be bringing her dogs and cats to claw up the curtains and rugs and run around in Father's house when I'm gone."

My pa was leaning over her by the bed, and he stood up now, an expression that looked like panic on his face.

My papa was the grandson of Bale Matthew McKinsey. He had never expected to get anything of Grandpa's, and I think the prospect of inheriting the beautiful big house was overwhelming him with expectation, although he was totally aware that Aunt Virginia Stockton may never let it happen. Perhaps the best thing would be to sell the property and divide the money fairly among all of the children. Yet, it was certainly a beautiful house. And in Papa's mind he was probably saying to himself, *Why should we live in the M&M Grocery store when we could live here?*

"Well, Aunt Selby, you know that I have to go back to Bremerton to finish up my work at the Navy yard. I wouldn't be here. It would be Frances and the girls, Lindy, Elaine, and Sylvia."

She turned her head back to look at my mother, and I took a good look at Mother then, who stood with the popsicle sticks in her hands and a perfectly stunned expression of absolute surprise on her face.

"Frances is such a good housekeeper," Selby Blue said. "And all of the little girls are such dear children to help her."

My father looked numb. Mother, the popsicle sticks looking precarious in her hands, elbowed him. "Tell her of course we'll come," she said, trying not to be too excited about living in a mansion. "Of course we'll come, Christmas tree or not."

He leaned back over Aunt Selby Blue and put a hand on

her arm. "Selby, are you sure you want young children around you? You must know we would do everything we can do to help you." After a pause, he said, "I think you're right about one thing. I'm sure Aunt Virginia will not show up if we're living here."

Aunt Selby didn't have to say anything after that. She just smiled and leaned back on the pillow. She held her hands out for the popsicle sticks and said, "Now fetch me the glue in the second drawer. Thank you."

5

As soon as we got in the car to go back, my father and mother began plotting how they would sell the yellow stucco house on State Street and the little store attached to it. My mother said we ought to list it with Papa's cousin Chandler Stockton, because Aunt Virginia would be coming down to snoop around if we moved into the mansion. My father said he didn't care. He bought the house from Bill Brown and he would list it with Bill Brown.

"I don't know how good at real estate these cousins are, and I know Mr. Brown," he said. "He's a good real estate agent. He can also help us buy a house in Denver, Colorado, if we go," my father said. He had still been thinking about working for the Bureau of Reclamation as a civil engineer. The government had offered him a job in Denver drawing plans for the spillways on the Hoover Dam.

As we went back to our house, I remembered we hadn't bought a Christmas tree. Elaine was the only one who made a fuss about it.

"We forgot the Christmas tree," she said.

"But Aunt Selby's allergic to pine needles. And we're going to be moving in with Aunt Selby very soon," my mother said. She got out a Christmas book and began reading it to the two little girls. I wasn't interested, and went into the other room and began drawing cartoons on a pad of old yellow paper.

We began packing the next day. My father borrowed a truck from the Stewarts and one of their boys helped him lift the dressers and beds into it. We drove over to Aunt Selby Blue's several times and packed everything we owned into her little garage.

I couldn't believe we were moving out of the M&M Grocery. Only a week after we listed it, someone by the name of Milton Hansen bought it and changed the second letter to H. Those last few days before we moved, I kept walking about looking at everything as though it might be the last time I would see it.

On the last night we would ever spend in the M&M, we slept on blankets on the floor. It was colder than ice in the house. Daddy had already told the gas company to turn off the gas, and the new owners hadn't turned it on yet. We burned wood in the tiny stove. The next day around noon I was very glad to pick up the blankets and the suitcases and get in the car to go to Aunt Selby's.

We had been talking to my dad's aunt every day, briefly. She had not changed her mind, but continued to say how happy she was that we were coming. She was sorry she was allergic to pine needles, but she was making a Christmas tree for us out of popsicle sticks.

I was so excited. Not about the tree made out of popsicle sticks. But about making up my bed in the little front bedroom upstairs that Mother said I could have for my own. She and

Daddy would have the larger front bedroom with the bay window. The girls would take the back upstairs bedroom.

But on that afternoon we drove to the mansion, we saw something that filled my mother with dread. She put her hands up to her mouth and ducked as though she were hiding herself. In the driveway of the old house, there was a car we had never seen before. A very sleek car decorated with chrome. It must have been a Lincoln. Inside the dark windows, we could see several dogs jumping up and down on the upholstery.

My father waited for a few minutes before we went up to the door. "Leave your things here for now. And just be calm. If it's Virginia, remember she can't do anything without Aunt Selby's permission."

But my mother shuddered. "Do you think she'll give us trouble, Bill?"

"Nobody can give you trouble if you don't take it," Papa said.

6

When we knocked on the mansion door, the first thing we saw was the bouffant hairdo. It appeared in the cut glass window and bobbed around for a moment under the blue and gold grapes twinkling in the afternoon sun.

My father looked at us and smiled. He was stomping about with his hands in his pockets. "Well, we'll just take it a step at a time," he said.

When the door opened, we saw Aunt Virginia Stockton for the first time. Her head looked like one of those garden mulberry trees that has been cut like a lollipop. She had the same fuzzy white hair as her sister Aunt Selby Blue. But perhaps because she was standing instead of lying on a pillow, she not only looked like a skinny tree, but a tall tree. I had to look up so far I thought I would wreck my neck. And in her arms was a scrawny white poodle shaved to the skin, with fuzzy fluff on his forehead. He looked at us out of tiny blue eyes and yawned.

"What do you think you're doing, Bill?" Virginia said. "Why, when I got wind of it, I came down immediately."

Daddy stood very patiently with his hand on the door. "Selby asked us to come in. We'll take good care of her," he said.

"I can't believe you would agree to such madness. She is a sick woman. She ought to be in the hospital."

There was a long pause, and then a small voice called from the back room, "Come on in, Bill."

"There is nothing you can do here that I can't do," Virginia said. "Three children will wreck this house."

My father took his hand off the doorknob and put one of his feet over the threshold. He practically walked into Virginia. The rest of us followed him.

Aunt Virginia Stockton was dressed in a black silk skirt and a white blouse with a high collar. Her stockings were black, and she wore large high-heeled shoes. "I don't think you know what you are doing. I was so shocked at Selby's behavior. She's not in her senses. I'm sorry, but she won't be able to handle your children."

"I think Selby Blue wanted someone to be with her at Christmastime," Pa said. He said the words with just enough bite to them that Virginia backed away as we walked into the hall. When we walked back to Selby's room to say hello, Virginia followed us with the poodle in her arms.

"I'm so glad you're here. Virginia just came to wish me Merry Christmas," Selby said. She was sitting up in the bed with a metal tray on her lap, and little popsicle Christmas trees marching across the tray. They were quite cute, with several layers of popsicle sticks glued together like scalloped skirts.

My pa looked out the door at Aunt Virginia, who stood so still she looked like a French impressionistic painting.

"We'll take it from here," Pa said to Virginia.

Elaine was still jumping up and down with glee. She jumped up and down in front of the poodle, poking its feet and making faces. Sylvia was also trying to get into the act, reaching for the dog with her short arms.

"What does that mean, you'll take it from here?" Virginia said. "I'm wondering what you're thinking?"

"We'll be all right," Mother said. "Really, we will. It's Christmastime. If you wish to stay with Aunt Selby, you are welcome."

Mother always tried to assign the best of motives to people. But Virginia wasn't paying any attention to her. "I've already talked to Chandler and Evelyn," she said. "I'll be in Salt Lake City for a few weeks until we go over some estate planning. I don't know what you're thinking, but Selby has no right to give this house to anyone. It belongs in the family. We have drawn up legal documents. George Crookston, Mayor of Provo, is one of my lawyers, and he understands all of the ramifications. I can see you've moved in here on account of Selby. But I'm telling you, she belongs in a nursing home. And that's what I am here to negotiate. If the children do any damage to the woodwork . . ." she paused. "I just want you to know you won't be here long. And I will have the courts on my side."

"We'll see," my pa said. "We'll see." And he walked her to the door.

"Oh, thank you, Bill," Aunt Selby said when we saw her in the back room lying on the bed. She was holding onto one of her milknickel-stick Christmas trees in one hand, and her nose with the other. "That's a cute little dog, but I was afraid I was going to sneeze."

7

As we went back out to the car to carry in our things, Mother was very quiet. When Papa unlocked the trunk and began dragging out the suitcases, she leaned toward him and whispered, "Do you think we ought to go ahead with this? I mean, I wonder if Virginia can get Selby into a nursing home after all, and take over? Do we have any proof Selby owns the house? To hear Virginia speak, the house still belongs to the family, and there isn't any legal right even for Selby to be here."

My father seemed to listen, but he didn't stop pulling the suitcases out of the trunk. "All I see is that Selby needs someone around her who cares. For now, let's just take it a step at a time."

He went back and forth, making several trips for the heavy suitcases. Each of us girls had a little Rainbow Bread bag full of our toothbrushes and socks and underwear. We carried them upstairs into the rooms we had already been assigned. The staircase was dark polished wood with a burgundy-colored runner up the middle. The banister was as thick as my waist, and the pilasters as bulbous and curved as any I had ever seen in a Victorian house. My room was at the top of the stairs. I had never seen it before this, but I had imagined every inch of it for the last few weeks. I gasped. It was even more spectacular than I had imagined. Both the narrow front window that I had seen from the street, and the window on the north, were draped with old peach-colored lace and heavy brocade and satin drapes with gold-brocaded cornices. Behind the curtains was a wall covered with striped paper in pastels. A wainscoting of shiny dark wood separated the striped wallpaper from a complimentary design of peach- and rose-colored peonies.

When I first stood in the room and drank up the peach and gold and rose-colored flowers, I breathed in and thought I smelled a garden. But it was a garden of my mind. I fell in love with the room instantly, and could barely touch anything in it without a sense that I was desecrating something from the past that I had not yet earned the right to inhabit. I felt this way about every room of the house. Down the hall was a bathroom with peach-colored tile surrounding a claw-foot tub. When I met Elaine coming out of the bathroom, I asked her if she had washed her hands. Yes, she had, she said. She hadn't touched anything yet. Her hands were red and raw from rubbing.

Papa put our suitcases on the tops of our beds. There were two beds in the back bedroom where Elaine and Sylvia were to sleep. Their bedroom was not as formal as the two front ones—mine, and the master bedroom next to me where Mother and Father would sleep. The girls' room had been Beauregard's, so it seemed a little stilted and boyish, with a crown molding of dark wood and a hand-painted row of blue and white sailboats marching around on every blue wall.

"You'll have to be careful not to float away on the sea while you're asleep," Mother joked with Elaine and Sylvia. Elaine was ecstatic with the space in the room after we had been cramped into the house we had owned at the M&M. She was pumping her arms up and down, up and down as she danced all over the dark blue carpet. A couple of throw rugs on the floor were knit with kittens in straw baskets. She wouldn't step on the kittens, but danced around them with glee. She named them. "This is Tinkerbell," she sang, "and this is St. Nicholas." I didn't argue with her, although I did not think the cat looked like Santa Claus. I supposed she was getting into the Christmas spirit.

After we had put our things carefully in the closets, Mother brought up a few of the Christmas decorations we had saved from years in the past.

"This is a perfect house for Christmas," she said. "Pick out something you want to put up in your room."

I chose a little brass star on a string, and hung it on the clasp that kept the window shut. It hung down just below the dark wood frame of the window, so that when I went outside, I could see it hanging there. I thought, *A star means many things.* I could not help but wonder what it would mean to us here, in our new surroundings.

8

There was a school across the street. We wanted to stay at Maeser, but the school board said no, and we couldn't walk all the way through town. So for the last few days before Christmas vacation began, we went to the new school. We didn't know anyone, and it wasn't easy, but we were able to walk home as soon as the bell rang. We always found Mother in the kitchen baking things for Aunt Selby: apples with cinnamon, potatoes, or whole wheat bread.

Elaine continued to bounce in pure rapture through the new house for the next couple of days. She helped Aunt Selby paint the milknickel-stick Christmas trees with green food coloring and place them on the wall dividers in the hall.

When I went upstairs to shut myself in the room, finish my homework, or read, I often heard her running up and down the stairs. I had to close my door to shut out the sound. I lay on the bed in front of my draped window with my book, and tried to concentrate. Mother would call to Elaine from the kitchen to come and help her take the food tray to Aunt Selby. She didn't really need Elaine's help; she did it just to stop her from running up and down, up and down. Mother had her hands full with the baby always at her feet, hanging to her legs.

Finally, on Friday afternoon, I was so tired of hearing Elaine's feet out in the hall that I decided I would find a place to read in the attic. I didn't care how dusty it was. I would rather have quiet.

On the first day we were in the house, we had stopped to look at the attic door in the hallway. My father had opened it. All we found was an old dusty wooden stairway that climbed to a small landing. There were boxes on the landing. My father said the attic was full of Aunt Sadie's old things, and we should just leave them alone.

The boxes on the landing were enough to discourage us from going upstairs. That is, until one particular day.

When I opened the door, it creaked so loud I thought Mother and Elaine would hear me. But they were in the kitchen making cookie dough. I had too much homework to help. Aunt Selby was asleep. The boxes were still sitting on the landing exactly as they had been when we looked at them last time. But this time I was curious, and I wanted to see the rest of the stairway. Selby had told us there were two rooms upstairs.

I tucked my books under my arm, climbed to the first step, and pulled the door to the stairs shut behind me. It didn't close completely because it had been warped or swollen by a hundred years of moisture, but it closed enough to stay shut. I was closed in, and I was hoping Elaine wouldn't find me.

There was thick dust on the stairs along with little pieces of paper that looked like price tags. Someone had cut the tags off their merchandise and let them drop.

The boxes said, FRAGILE and EXPRESS in big white tags pasted in several places. There was one open box of papers filed sideways so that you could see the backs of several little booklets. They were labeled, *Lolita Mercedes Humphreys Chamberlain, Volume 1, 2, 3* and on up to *10*. I didn't dare take one out to see what it was.

There was a box of hats stacked one on top of the other, and a piece of fur that looked like the tail of a fox. I didn't touch that because it looked alive.

In order to go past the landing, I had to turn and step over the box of papers and a crate. There was a turn to the left and about three more steps that went up to another landing. At the top of that landing were two doors facing each other. The right one that led to the room at the front of the house was ajar.

9

I wasn't quite sure how brave I wanted to be. But I dared to touch the door to see if it would open further. It moved about two inches and then something stopped it. It looked like it could have been a ghost. But of course I didn't believe in ghosts. I was wise to the ways of the world. Ghouls and phantoms were only creatures of the imagination.

But when the door stopped, a chill went up my back. A clear image began filtering through to me from the other side of the door. I thought I could see an old man—maybe it was Grandfather Bale Matthew McKinsey—sitting in an old rocking chair and watching me through his spectacles. And when I had tried to come into the room, he had just put out his foot, clad in a heavy leather boot, and stopped me from opening the door.

I could see that the inside of the room was dark, with boxes and trunks and old pieces of furniture. There was an old dressing table standing close by. It had originally been painted blue, and someone had painted yellow over that. And someone else had tried to sand the yellow away. I saw a face in the mirror, and I gasped. But then I realized the face was mine. I turned my head this way and that and thought it was time I had a haircut.

When I looked further back in the room I could see there was a window with a few chinks of light in it. The big trees in front of the mansion were bobbing against the triangles of sky. The rest of the window was boarded up with old cardboard. The window must have been broken many years ago and Aunt Selby had pasted an old box over most of it because she hadn't been able to afford to replace it with glass.

There was just enough light to outline some of the shapes in the room, and when my eyes got used to the darkness, I began to see the old chairs piled up on one another, a couple of old dressers with drawers, a bedstead, and boxes of old hats and toys, and books. One box was overflowing with old boots and shoes.

I was fascinated. I thought to myself that there couldn't have been any treasure greater than a box of old books. And the wheels in my head began turning, making plans for a Christmas-vacation reading marathon. I would come upstairs where no one else would know I was, and I could read these books to my heart's content.

I hadn't stepped into the room yet, although the door was open enough that I could probably get in without pushing at Grandfather Bale Matthew McKinsey's foot if he were indeed sitting in a rocking chair behind the door. So I ventured across the threshold to see if I could look at the titles of some of the books in the boxes. But as soon as I put my head in the door, I backed up quicker than a body could say *Jack Robinson*. My heart pounded like a jack hammer. In a far corner of the room off to the left I saw a flowing white figure. And I could swear it was moving.

10

My mouth was so dry, I couldn't even yell. I backed up so quickly on the landing that I slipped down the steps and into the packing boxes behind me.

I knew there were no such things as ghosts. At least, I thought I knew. But I also knew I had seen the white towering object at the back of the room sway. And when I had combined my vision of Grandfather Bale Matthew McKinsey behind the door, and the ghost in the dresser mirror, the third phantom had just been so real that it had taken me by surprise. I didn't move from the stoop. The light from the window on the stairs was strong enough to let me read my homework, so I tried to pull out my history assignment and look at it, as I had intended to do.

But my mind had shut down. I couldn't read a word. I had seen that white thing moving. I knew it. It looked like a ghost. I wanted to laugh at myself, but as I sat there shaking, I was totally aware that it might be entirely possible that a ghost lived in this house. I shuddered and slipped quietly down the stairs. At the doorway to the second floor hallway, I listened before I opened the door. When I was sure I couldn't hear anyone, I crept out and shut it.

"Where have you been?" came Elaine's squeaky little voice. I looked behind me. She had been coming up the stairs. I didn't think she had seen me until I had come out of the attic.

"Where did you go, Lindy?" she said. "Mother wants you to help us make Christmas cookies. Then we'll take them to the neighbors."

"I've been trying to do my homework," I said. I was right by the bathroom, so I made some excuse about having a stomach-ache.

"Well, come and help us. We rolled out a dozen cookies. We have enough dough for a couple dozen snowmen. You can help us put frosting and eyes and mouths on them."

I could only hope that it hadn't registered with Elaine that I had been snooping around upstairs. She would tell Mother and that would be the end of it.

I followed Elaine downstairs to the kitchen, my heart beating so fast that I could hear it bump against my ribs.

"Lindy has a stomach-ache," she announced to my mother.

"Oh, I'm sorry," Mother said.

I could have imagined a real enough stomach-ache after what had appeared in the upstairs room. But I wasn't going to look like a stupid idiot. "It's all right now."

"Well, help us frost the ones that are coming out of the oven," my mother said. "We'll have enough cookies to take some to our old friends on State Street."

We frosted enough cookies that afternoon to fill Santa's sleigh. While we were fending off baby Sylvia's advances on the red hots and green frosting for the Christmas trees, Elaine asked Mother several times, "Can't we ever get a real Christmas tree?"

Because Mother didn't answer right away, I told Elaine, "Just don't ask about the Christmas tree."

But she ignored me completely. So after the third time Elaine asked the question, Mother said, "Remember, there are some problems about having a Christmas tree. Let's just get as many of these cookies done as we can. We have some guests coming early this afternoon, and I want to give them a large plate to take home with them."

We worked for another three hours.

11

After we had frosted a few more snowmen white and decorated them with raisin eyes, we found out from Mother just who was supposed to be coming this afternoon. It was strange that she didn't really want to tell us. She hemmed and hawed. When we finally got it out of her, she said the names softly in a little twist of her mouth, as though she didn't want us to hear anything. "It's Chandler and Evelyn Stockton," she said.

"Why are they coming?" I wanted to know. I smelled a rat. "What's going on? I thought Selby Blue was not going to sell her house?"

"They are Aunt Virginia's son and daughter-in-law, you know. Aunt Selby is their aunt, too."

"I know that," I said. I had paid particular attention to the details of all the relationships. "But Daddy said they are in the real estate business."

"So?" Mom said. "Everyone has to earn a living somehow."

"Not that," I kept after her. "Daddy said they never come to visit Aunt Selby unless they want something."

"Lindy, it's Christmas," my mother told me. "Can't you just accept that maybe what they want is to wish us and Aunt Selby a Merry Christmas?"

It frustrated me that Mother was always so positive about everyone, while I still remembered Virginia's teeth showing when she said, "I just want you to remember you won't be here long. I have the courts on my side." Now it seemed that Virginia was sending her vanguard troops to sweep us out.

Again, Elaine wanted to know if Daddy was going to bring home a Christmas tree for the occasion. Daddy told her Aunt Selby would cough if there were a Christmas tree, but she kept asking why they couldn't just close the door. Sylvia listened and toddled around and around a kitchen stool, hitting it with the open palm of her right hand.

"Aunt Selby can't breathe around pine needles. We want to take good care of Aunt Selby. She's taking good care of us."

Again we were reminded we had left the Christmas tree lot without getting a tree and had come to Aunt Selby's to rescue her, and now there would be no Christmas tree.

When mother said "needles," I thought she said "noodles," and I turned around to ask her about it, and found a gray face framed in a white ruffle looming in the doorway. Since I had just seen a ghost upstairs, I was a bit jumpy, and I started when I saw the face in the bed-cap. It was Aunt Selby.

"Look at the cookies!" Aunt Selby said, smiling. She had flung her blanket around her shoulders, and her feet were bare.

34

"Selby!" Mother said. "You aren't supposed to get up. Get back in bed immediately. I didn't hear your bell ringing." Mother flew around to the other side of the table and tried to usher Selby back to the bedroom. But she wouldn't go.

"I know. Chandler and Evelyn are coming. Bill told me. That is nice of you to make cookies for them. What nice cookies," Aunt Selby said. "I remember when I was a little girl, we made cookies at this very same table and my papa would come in and eat the biggest one. He would laugh and say that we'd better hide them or he would eat them all."

I tried to look at Aunt Selby with different eyes. It was hard to imagine that she was a young girl once who liked to make cookies.

"I heard you talking about the tree," Aunt Selby said. "Remember, I told you I have a Christmas tree somewhere in the house," Selby said. "I wanted to tell you where it was, but I haven't put it up the last few years. So I've forgotten where it was. You are welcome to look for it. I made it when Seymour died, and I've used it every year. It's made out of macaroni."

Mother looked at Aunt Selby. I saw her just about drop a handful of raisins in the bowl of green frosting. Her eyes opened up and she stopped for a few minutes, just to think about what Aunt Selby was saying. "Okay, sure," she finally got out. "A macaroni Christmas tree. Well, I'll send the girls to find it."

I froze. It was certainly clear that Aunt Selby hadn't had a Christmas tree for many years. I was pretty sure Mother was going to send me down into that gloomy cellar with the spiders to look for it. Or worse, the ghost-infested attic. I just sat there staring at Elaine, who had knocked the red hots across the table.

12

I was waiting for Mother to tell me to go down in the basement to find the macaroni Christmas tree, but she began bustling around the kitchen like a madwoman, getting the red hots picked up off the table and put into a dish so they wouldn't fall off while she got Aunt Selby safely back into her bed.

"You mustn't worry about the Christmas tree, or whether or not the children have one," Mother said to Aunt Selby as she took her elbow and turned her around. "They'll be fine. You really shouldn't be up, especially without three or four pairs of socks and your slippers on your feet."

As she took Selby down the hall, she kept up the chatter. "But thank you for telling us about the macaroni tree, and we'll see what we can do. Now you know that the Stocktons are coming in only a few minutes. We need to be ready for them, so we won't do the Christmas decorations for a while."

Aunt Selby didn't have a chance. I could barely hear her weak little voice. "I'd like to be up and in the living room if it would be all right." But the doctor had given his strict orders. And I think Mother had her own reasons that she wanted Aunt Selby in bed when the Stocktons came.

We watched at the window for their car. It wasn't long before a sleek new black Buick drove into the driveway. I had never seen such a big car. It was beautiful. There were chrome pieces along the edges by the wheels, across the hood and down the sides. The windows were tinted so dark that we could not see who was inside. It was a spectacular car, and I expected at any minute to see the mayor climb out of it, or the President of the United States.

But what we did see was just as interesting, if not more so. I assumed the woman who climbed out on our side was Evelyn Stockton. Like her mother-in-law, she was dressed in black as though she were attending a funeral. A little pillbox hat, frothy with netting, sat on top of her head. She wore such high heels, I was afraid she was going to topple over in them. Her suit was of a sleek and shiny material that glimmered in the afternoon light. But it was her face that I noticed most of all. Shading her face with her right hand, she squinted and looked from the top to the bottom of the house. And then she gave a little laugh. It must have been in response to something Mr. Stockton said, for he was out of the car now, and pointing to different parts of the house as though he had been explaining something important. He was dressed in a smart-looking blue wool blazer with a crest on the pocket. His pressed white shirt was so bright it looked like a blank piece of paper.

We tucked ourselves down in the couch in front of the window so they wouldn't see us. But my head stuck up far enough that I could still see Evelyn go to the back door of the fancy car, open it, and stand as though she were talking to somebody. Vaguely I could make out a dark head-sized shape that I hadn't noticed before. Though she stood there for a few moments discussing something of importance, the dark head never emerged. She was probably asking whoever it was to come in. But nothing happened. Finally, she shut the door with a sharp jab and joined her husband on the walkway to the porch. Her mouth was in a sour little line. When Mother saw us spying from behind the couch, she scolded us. Elaine and I got up off the floor and brushed the cookie flour off our hands to make ourselves presentable for the Stocktons.

13

"Hello, Evelyn and Chandler," my mother said. "We're so glad you could come." Sometimes I thought my mother was crazy. I was sure she couldn't have been "glad" they could come. But I knew all of this talk was just necessary social chatter, like grease in a machine. "Please come in," she said.

The weather had been good, so they didn't have big coats. When Mother asked if she could take their wraps, they insisted no, they could stay for only a short time. They would wear the blazer and the suit jacket in the house.

Although Chandler left his hands in his pants pockets, Evelyn shook a gloved hand with both of us and smiled. "It's nice to see you girls. My, you've grown! Are you having a nice Christmas? Oh, so Aunt Selby has made you some of her stick Christmas trees, I see. How lovely." Chandler had his eyes directed toward the bedroom, anxious to visit with Aunt Selby Blue.

I thought Aunt Evelyn was going to be rude and wicked. But I had to admit I thought she was very pretty, and quite gracious.

"We haven't started Christmas vacation yet," I said. "But we're trying to get in the spirit. We put the milk-nickel trees up in the hallway already, and we made cookies today. You can have some."

My mother looked at us with one of those "Please Get Lost" looks and said, "Why don't you girls go into the kitchen and make up a plate of cookies for the Stocktons?"

On the way out into the hall, I just glanced at the car in the driveway and its mysterious occupant, wondering if that person had decided to come in after all, when what did I see but disaster. The shadow-head had changed from the back seat to the driver's seat. And then I couldn't believe what occurred! The car was moving! In that moment that I stood at the oval window in the door, the car jerked forward, stopped, then jerked forward again. Mesmerized, I stood looking without a word. There was one last great jerk and the car raced forward toward the house full throttle! Right before my eyes, that shiny black Buick climbed a couple of steps on the porch before it stopped. And on its way, it was knocking and scattering bricks right and left like dominoes.

A big lump came up in my throat. I was watching the hunk of metal sit like a rock, and I realized there was no movement behind the tinted windshield. I could see someone's head lying against the upholstery. It seemed strange that I couldn't even move.

At first I was paralyzed, but in a moment I raced back into the hall that led to Selby's back bedroom. Aunt Evelyn and Uncle Stockton were following my mother back to see their aunt. The hallway was narrow enough that when I glanced back, all I could see was Chandler Stockton's huge back, with the blue blazer looking like a navy blue wall. When I peered

THE MACARONI CHRISTMAS TREE

around under his elbow I could see my mother busy at Selby's bedside with Aunt Virginia who was leaning over the bed saying, "Are you sure you can't find those documents? Didn't you know where Dad put them?"

I didn't feel much like pounding Chandler Stockton on the back to tell him what was going on. And I couldn't get through. "Mother," I called weakly. But she was so busy propping Selby up with pillows, that she could barely hear me. When I ducked under his elbow again and said, "Mother," she did look at me briefly, but her look definitely said, "I'm busy now." I was having a hard time.

Feeling as nervous as a decapitated chicken, I just wanted to run. I ran back to the front door and looked out. The head behind the tinted window was still resting on the upholstery in the same place. Somebody ought to find out if the person inside the car was still alive. And it was probably going to be me. I opened the door and slipped outside.

42

14

Walking to the car smashed up against the bricks of Aunt Selby's porch seemed like the longest walk I had ever made in my life. I cautiously came around to the driver's side and peeked in. The head was still there, attached to the rest of the body, and looking quite unconscious. Feeling afraid, I knocked on the window. The head moved very slightly. So I opened the car door.

"Are you all right?" I asked.

The head turned toward me and one eye opened just enough to take a look at me. "Mmmmph," the head said. It was a good-sized boy dressed in a blazer like his dad's, with a huge crest on the pocket. The boy was about my age or a little older, probably about thirteen or fourteen. His hair, choppy and dark, was standing on top of his head as if he had been electrocuted. He had heavy brows like his father, and firm large jowls. His nose seemed small for his face; his lips were slick as though he were drooling. He made noises that came out of his nose more than his mouth. Finally, forming words with his big slick lips, he groaned, "I'm dying."

I wanted to make the standard reply we had always made in our family, "Isn't everybody?" We had always made a point of emphasizing the transitory nature of every single life force on earth, whether it be plant or animal. We were indisputably

43

all on our way to the ultimate—the afterlife. Mother would always say, "This is your lifetime here and you are who you are, so where are you going? Every day counts. You make the choices." It would definitely count as a bad day for Virginia's son, but it was obvious that he himself had chosen it.

"How old are you?" I said.

"Other than being almost dead, fourteen," he said.

That's what I thought. He was a couple of years older than I was. "Can you move your legs?"

For a moment he closed his eyes and I could see he was sending some kind of electrical messages to his knees. They twitched and then moved slightly.

"You must have pushed the wrong pedal," I said.

"Oh really!" he said, sitting up and looking at the bricks falling away from the porch. "Oh no!" and he wiped his drippy nose and lips with the sleeve of his blazer. "I've done it now! I'm dead. You, whoever you are . . ." He looked at me for the first time, opening his eyes and then closing them again. "You're looking at a dead man."

"I already tried to get your dad, but he's busy right now. Shall I try to fetch him again?"

"Don't you dare tell my dad what I did."

I could see right away that keeping this mishap a secret from his parents was going to be impossible. But I would honor his request. There was no way I would be the one to tell. I was sure his dad would just be glad he wasn't killed. While I stood there watching him, he had begun moving his legs and arms. Pretty soon he was wild as a windmill, making such exuberant discomfort noises that his spit landed in my hair. I opened the door wide while he tried to get out of the car.

15

I was glad I didn't have to say a word to the parents. I
didn't have to. Elaine had come out of the kitchen and pressed
her nose against the front window. I saw her out of the corner
of my eye. Sylvia was there too, pushing her sticky hands
against the glass. And then Elaine had disappeared, and I knew
she had probably run into Selby's bedroom and tugged on Mr.
Stockton's blue blazer. And I was right.

Now she was running out the front door in front of all the
parents, pointing to the car and chirping, "See, see!" And
suddenly the dad, Chandler Stockton, managed to metamor-
phose the red of his face into all shades of white and gray. For
a moment he stood frozen on the porch as though he had seen
a ghost. When Evelyn came up behind him, she screamed. Her
scream moved Chandler to action. He ran down the steps and
toward the driver's seat of the car. "Stupid! Rochester!" he
yelled. "What have you done? You stupid idiot!" he yelled.

"Oh, my goodness," my mother said. She ran behind
Evelyn and hurried to the boy in the driver's seat. "Are you all
right?" she said, putting her hand on his brow.

I stood back, analyzing these statements and their
sources. Evelyn had just gone nuts, Chandler had seen the car
and had gone ballistic, and only my mother was worried about
the boy, whose name I had just learned, was Rochester. I felt

sorry for him. He had certainly committed a no-no. But there didn't seem to be anyone in his family who would show him any empathy. And I was sure he would be sore after the crash.

Rochester promptly closed his eyes. "I'm dying," he said.

"Merry Christmas. Aren't we all," Chandler Stockton said. And I knew he had either heard my mother say it, or my mother got it from my father and his family. "You make the choices."

16

Rochester wasn't happy to get out of the car. He limped and moaned. But his father insisted he get out. And after Rochester was removed from the driver's seat, Evelyn and Mother flanked him on both sides and helped him back into the house. I didn't think anything was seriously wrong with him. He was just shaken up and ornery.

Chandler Stockton got back into the car, started the motor, and backed it up into the driveway again where it belonged. The car would run perfectly. It just had a tremendous dent in the right front fender.

Following Rochester and my mother and Evelyn into the house, I looked once more at the bricks and wondered who was going to fix them. There were about five bricks so broken they would have to be replaced, and I wondered if there were a way to buy new bricks that would match them.

Mother and Evelyn put Rochester on the front sofa and brought him orange juice and hot chicken soup. They were making a big fuss over him while we just stood in the background, hoping not to be noticed.

Finally, Mother said, "It's time to look for Aunt Selby's Christmas tree. It would be nice to put up the Christmas decorations before the Stocktons go."

I couldn't believe her. What did she need Christmas decorations for when there was a brick wall to put together, an old lady dying in the back bedroom, and a boy claiming he's about dead on the front sofa?

I guess Mother just needed some cheer. But for me, it was an invitation to suffer through a lot of nervous tension. I wasn't very excited about going down into the dark damp basement without knowing what was down there, or up into the stuffy attic where I was sure I had seen a ghost.

"Go on, now. You and Elaine go look for that macaroni Christmas tree."

We were in the front room and Rochester was still on the sofa. When Mother said something about the macaroni Christmas tree, he opened one of his eyes. He looked out of it warily. It looked like a perfectly healthy eye to me. I thought he would be opening the other one in a moment. And I was right.

"Macaroni Christmas tree?" he muttered. "That mangy-looking Christmas tree she always brings out every year?" So Rochester had seen it before.

"That's probably the one," Mother said.

"I think I know where it is," Rochester said.

I felt a wave of relief. "Well, then, Rochester can help us find it," I said.

"Oh, sure. I probably know where it is," Rochester said. He sounded perfectly healthy, and I thought to myself, we'll let *him* go up in the attic and discover the ghost. We'll let *him* muck around in the damp basement.

"He's just been in quite a crash," Mother said. "I'm not sure we should ask him to get up just yet."

"No, I'm okay," Rochester said, though a few moments before, he had announced his demise.

It took a few more minutes for Rochester to get up on his feet. He sat up on the sofa for a minute, pushing the hair out of his eyes. Aunt Evelyn had been in the back bedroom explaining what had happened to Aunt Selby. When she came out and saw Rochester sitting up, she was alarmed.

"No, Rochester, you shouldn't be getting up. What are you doing?"

"They want the macaroni Christmas tree."

"That can wait," Evelyn said.

"No, we'll do it now. I'm all right," Rochester said.

Evelyn was quiet—as though she never let herself argue with Rochester.

Rochester suddenly got up, and lumbering like a big ape who wasn't sure how to move every part of a body that had grown out of control, he started up the stairs.

17

As we walked up the stairs behind Rochester, we heard some talking in the hall. It was Mr. Stockton in a clandestine conversation with his wife Evelyn. He didn't see us waiting on the upper landing of the staircase, and we caught the drift of his speech.

"Maybe now that the house is a wreck it will be better for us to take it over from Selby," Chandler said.

"I don't know. Aren't there some papers somewhere? Your mother says there are some papers somewhere that tell exactly who the house goes to. Only Selby knows where they are," Evelyn said.

"Those papers have been missing for years," Chandler said.

"They're not in any safe, or bank deposit box?"

"No. But we know the old man drew them up and Selby agreed to them. We're pretty sure they give the house to the oldest child."

"You can't be sure until we find them."

"I'm not going to fix the porch. It can stay wrecked until it gets into our hands," Chandler said.

"That's all right," Evelyn replied. "At least don't worry about it."

Rochester had opened the door to the attic now. I hurried away from the staircase and into the long hall. Elaine was following him, too, and I tried to get her out of the way.

"Elaine, there isn't room in the attic for a lot of people," I told her. "You'd better not go."

"Aw, let her come," Rochester said. "The more the merrier."

Then I told him: "I think there's ghosts up there."

"Oh, yeah?" Rochester said from the stairwell. His words echoed against the walls.

"Yes. I was up there not long ago and I saw a ghost," I said.

"All the more reason we should all stick together," he said.

I could barely hear him, he was so far away from us, now. And then I could not hear him at all. I wondered if he had already opened the door and gone in.

The boxes on the upstairs landing were still sitting in the same places with their signs: EXPRESS and AIR MAIL.

Nothing had been touched since I had been here a few days ago. When we couldn't hear Rochester anymore, Elaine backed down a step.

"What's the matter?" I asked her.

"Rochester's not up there anymore," Elaine told me. "The ghost gobbled him up."

"Aw! There can't be any such a thing as ghosts," I said, although I was not at all certain that she wasn't absolutely correct. We hadn't heard any of the doors open, and we weren't hearing any sound at all now.

Suddenly, as though it were ice, a cold feeling gripped my neck. I had been so sure there were no such things as ghosts, I wasn't looking for ghosts, I didn't want ghosts to appear from anywhere. And yet in that moment I wasn't convinced that such a phenomenon as ghosts wasn't a reality. I felt like my hair was standing on end.

18

Elaine hadn't been to see the ghost in the front room of the attic, and I didn't want her to feel the grip of fear that I felt. So I put on a big act. Just for her.

"Oh, everything's all right. There's an explanation. Are you coming or not?" I asked her.

She froze like a popsicle.

"Let's just go up and find out where he is," I said.

She didn't say a word. But she was still backing down the stairs. However, I stood in her way so that she couldn't get through.

"He's probably fainted or something," I told her. "Then it would be awful to leave him up here in the attic all by himself. Let's not make Uncle Chandler and Aunt Evelyn worried. Let's just go up and see where he is. He can't completely disappear."

Elaine was all limbs and they were all shaking. She was like a long-legged bird when I touched her thin bones. And she was frightened.

"Here, I'll hold your hand," I said. I put my arm around her trembling shoulders and we walked slowly up the stairwell.

Elaine may have been afraid, but I was almost terrified. I had never breathed a word to her that when I had investigated this area, I had seen the ghost in the front attic bedroom.

Climbing the stairs under these circumstances was a slow business. But we managed to get a few steps from the top where the boxes had begun piling up. When we reached the boxes, I could hear a low, almost inaudible whistling sound. The hair rose up on the back of my neck.

I didn't know if Elaine heard it, I didn't want to make anything of it, so I tried to shut down my ears. I didn't want to climb anymore stairs. I didn't want to get to the top and find Rochester dead with a whistling sound coming through his nose.

Elaine's bony hands tightened on my blouse. She had such a strong hold on me I couldn't have extricated myself if I had wanted to.

"Do you want to go back down by yourself?" I asked her.

"No," she said, her jaw clattering.

"Do you want to find the macaroni Christmas tree?"

"Yes," she said, her little teeth coming together like castanets in a Mexican band.

"Well, then, let's just keep going until we find the macaroni Christmas tree."

But when I urged her forward, she backed up against me and pushed her feet against the top stair where there were boxes hanging over the step and other boxes around the door.

"Well, go back down, then," I said.

"No, no," she whined. Her little legs were like fossilized chicken feet.

"Well, I can't wait up here forever," I said, "just because you don't want to move. At least we'd better find out what happened to Rochester."

Then we heard not only the whistle, but a thin piercing sound like the holler of a ghost. It was terrible. Every bit of my blood seemed to turn instantly cold.

"Ooooooooh," the muffled sound said. "Oooooooh."

Elaine jerked back into my arms and again stiffened her legs. I turned around so fast, the stairs were a blur. Half-dragging her down the stairs with me, I ran—down the steps, down into the second floor hallway, and down onto the large staircase that went to the first floor. I ran into the kitchen where Mother was getting ready to fix dinner.

We were so out of breath, my mother looked startled. "What has happened?" she asked.

"Oh, nothing," I said. "We couldn't find the macaroni Christmas tree in the attic."

"But that's where Aunt Selby thinks she put it when she used it last," Mother said.

"Rochester is still trying," I said.

19

Mother was peeling potatoes and asked me if I would please take over, since she had some dough to make up for rolls she was planning on having for supper.

"Why are we having such a fancy supper?" I asked. "Are Aunt Evelyn and Uncle Chandler staying?"

"Yes, they've agreed to stay to supper with us," Mother said. "Chandler and Evelyn have gone out to get a bid on the body of the car. The fender was smashed to smithereens."

I knew that. But it was stranger to me, still, that Uncle Chandler and Aunt Evelyn were so quick to begin fixing the fender on the car, when their own son might have fainted in the attic and needed a tune up in a different way, but every bit as important.

We didn't have to wait long for Rochester. In a few moments he came down into the kitchen. He lumbered like a big sack of sand. And I thought his face looked very white.

"So, did you chicken out?" he said to me. "Where did you and Elaine go so fast? You never came up to look with me."

Mother was standing with her back to us kneading a pile of bread dough. She turned around and concentrated on

Rochester's face. "You ought to sit down. You're still flushed, Rochester. Oh, I hope this accident hasn't caused any permanent damage."

"I'm all right," Rochester said. But he sat on a kitchen chair at the table right over the Christmas cookies, and began looking at them with longing.

"Go ahead and have a cookie," Mother said. "If you feel all right. And if it doesn't spoil your dinner."

He must have felt all right, for he had four. As he sat there eating one cookie after another, Mother began asking him questions. What school did he go to? What did he want to be? Those kinds of questions.

"I go to the Wood River Private School," he said. "I want to play football on television."

"I thought you played it on a football field," Elaine said. Both of us were sitting there watching him eat cookies. We were so upset by the ghosts in the attic that we didn't eat anything.

"Dummy," Rochester said, though he said it in a good natured way.

"You want to be a professional football player?" my mother asked, her back still to us as she kneaded the bread dough on the kitchen counter.

"I'm going to play for Harvard first," he said. "When we get this house sold we'll have enough money to send me anywhere I want to go."

"You're going to sell the house?" Mother said, surprised.

"Of course. You don't think we'd live *here*, do you?"

"Well, I don't know if the house will go to you, Rochester. Have you ever thought that if we found those papers your great grandfather Bale drew up, that he might not have given the house to your parents?"

"Yeah. I've thought about that. My dad says not to worry about it, the mayor has some pull, and we have some pull with the mayor. We can get the house."

While Rochester was stuffing the last cookie into his mouth, I turned away. He looked like a big piggy stuffing that whole cookie with frosting and red hots and silver sprinkles between his teeth. After he had a big chunk of Christmas cookie in his mouth, he came down hard on it and seemed to gulp it before he had a chance to get a good taste. I thought he looked like a vacuum cleaner.

"Well, let's put the cookies away," Mother said. So we did.

20

Uncle Chandler and Aunt Evelyn came back with a man in a red tow truck. They were leaving their car at the QUICK SERVICE Auto Body and Repair. Mr. Hooper, the man who ran the QUICK SERVICE was a big lumbering red-headed fellow with pock-marked cheeks and a stub of a cigar in his mouth. He drove the Stocktons back from the garage in his truck, and when he dropped them off at the curb, he decided to get out and come around to look at the brick wall. We stood in the yard and watched. I thought maybe he did walls as well as cars, for he was very intense in the way he picked up the bricks and looked at them, and tried to put them back together like pieces of a puzzle.

"Well, my brother can do this," Mr. Hooper said, chewing on the end of the cigar. There was no smoke coming out of the cigar, so it looked as though he chewed it to have some tobacco in his mouth. "Do you want me to send my brother by?"

"No, not yet," Mr. Stockton said. "We'll wait for a while and see what's going to happen." He said the next sentence under his breath, "You know, we have an old aunt in the house who's ready to die any day. When she's gone, we'll see whose house this is. And who's responsible."

"We have to find the papers," Evelyn reminded him.

"Yes, we still haven't found the papers," Chandler said in a guttural voice as though he were trying to ignore the truth.

"Well, when you get ready, let me know," the man with the cigar butt said. "I'll have your car ready probably in two weeks."

"If that's the best you can do, that's the best you can do," Chandler said.

As Mr. Hooper turned and walked toward the red tow truck, I thought he looked like a big knot. All of his muscles glistened in the sun. He had huge arms and legs. His striped tee shirt was so tight it rode up his belly.

All of us stayed out in the yard, waiting for the tow truck to drive away. It was still good weather for December, and though we rubbed our arms to ward off the cold, the sun was still shining in the sky. However, no sooner had the tow truck taken off than we saw a sleek navy blue limousine coming down the street. At first I thought it was Aunt Virginia's car, but Chandler began walking toward the street. "It's the mayor," he said. "Mother's attorney!"

There was an almost audible gasping sound, as though everybody breathed in at the same time. At first I didn't see two people behind dark windows, but when it pulled up to the curb I could see Aunt Virginia in the passenger side. A man I had never seen before was driving.

As we stood with our mouths hanging open, we also felt a sudden gust of wind, as though there was going to be a storm.

21

At the very same time the mayor and Virginia drove up in the limousine, it began to snow.

We hadn't seen much snow this winter yet. Elaine was ecstatic. Still in her stocking feet out on the sidewalk, watching the flakes fall down out of the sky like little bits of paper floating on the air, she danced like she had gone crazy. Leaning her head back, she stuck out her tongue to catch the little pieces of ice and swallow them.

"A white Christmas! A white Christmas!" Elaine laughed.

Mother put a coat on baby Sylvia and let her toddle out into the flurry. The snow began to fall in earnest. When Virginia stopped the car, she got out in the terrible wind, with the tiny snowflakes whirling about.

Even more interesting to me than Virginia was the man who sat behind the wheel of the big car. He was a distinguished-looking gentleman with a bald head. There didn't seem to be one strand of hair anywhere, and he wasn't wearing a hat. I thought he looked like a Christmas tree ornament. We didn't have a tree, but I had a fleeting thought that maybe we could have used him to decorate the house.

When he parked in the driveway and got out, he bowed slightly to Chandler and Evelyn who were in the process of coming into the mansion.

"Hello, Stocktons!" he greeted them. "So good to see you all the way down from Salt Lake City!"

"Isn't it nice they could come for Christmas," Virginia said. "But where is your car?"

Chandler Stockton appeared to stand on one foot and then on the other. "I was going to call you, Mother, but I knew you would be coming as soon as you possibly could." He hesitated and looked at the man with the bald head. "We had a small problem and sent the car to be repaired." He then changed the subject. "How nice that you could get the mayor to come our way."

My father Bill, my mother, and Evelyn Stockton turned around and greeted the man with hearty handshakes. "Hello, Mayor Crookston. What an honor! To what do we owe this visit?"

The mayor's bald head nodded and he half-bowed from his waist. "I'm so glad to be here," he announced.

"I suppose you haven't found the papers, then?" Virginia said to Chandler.

Chandler shook his head slowly.

"Well, there's a certain document that releases them and another that can be drawn up according to the wishes of the heirs. The mayor said he was willing to do that for us!"

"We can do it only if Mrs. Raine signs it," the mayor said.

"Oh, she'll comply," Virginia said.

"Well, then, it's not going to be difficult at all." He put out his arm as though to show Virginia the way. Since the snow was falling in earnest now, all of us ducked up the steps, through the huge door, and into the dark wood hall. Elaine and I and Rochester were the last ones, and Rochester shut the heavy door with a bang.

22

When the adults went into Selby's room, they shut the door.

Rochester almost followed them, but they closed him out just before he could get his foot in. He turned around to us with a scowl on his face and said, "This is to be my house. I don't know why I can't have a say-so."

It was to be his house? I felt a cold chill grab me under the hair and ripple down my back. "What do you mean it's to be *your* house?"

"Just that. My mother is the oldest in the family, and the house should go to her. Then I am to get the house. My older sister Jean got married and moved to Brighton, Massachusetts. She doesn't want the house, so I'm to live in it while I go to college."

I couldn't believe it. Just the look of disdain in his eyes was enough to freeze my ears.

"I don't think Aunt Selby is going anywhere," I said.

"Well, either hell or heaven," Rochester said.

I always wondered why everyone else didn't make up some place in between like I did. If you were just on the edge of belonging in hell, I was quite sure there was another place where you could practice coming up a notch.

Elaine didn't care. She began dancing up and down and singing Christmas carols. She ran into the kitchen where the cookies were and began eating cookies. Rochester was very generous with himself, and took almost half a dozen before we could gather them up to put into the cookie jar. I wasn't as worried about the cookies, however, as I was about a sound I heard far above us. I was sure I heard a cry of distress from somewhere up high. It sounded like Sylvia had fallen down somewhere upstairs.

Elaine, close to the doorway, made a dash up the stairway. And Rochester and I followed her. We found Sylvia at the bottom of the stairs to the attic, sitting in the hallway weeping buckets of tears.

"Up there!" Sylvia said. "Up there!"

"What happened up there? What are you talking about?"

"Bad lion up there."

Well, I had seen the ghost a couple of days ago and heard it moaning earlier in the day. But I had never seen a lion.

Rochester took up the challenge immediately. "No lion's up there," he said.

"Are you sure?" Elaine asked him. "She saw a lion."

"That is the biggest joke I've heard today." Rochester said. "There might be a green-eyed monster. But no lion."

Sylvia cried more tears.

"A green-eyed monster?" I asked him. "You're scaring the wits out of her. Just say there's nothing up there and go up to prove it." But when I put it to him that way, Rochester looked bleached. He looked at me as though his words had meant nothing at all. I wasn't going to back down, though.

"Okay, I'll do it," he said. "If you have a flashlight."

Oh, so he would do it *if he had a flashlight.* I thought he was demonstrating his cowardly side, and I wasn't sure how such a big boy could be such a panty waist. But I thought, *Okay, I'll play along to some extent,* and I went into Mom and Dad's bedroom and found the flashlight in the upper right-hand drawer.

There wasn't much of a light in it. But Rochester flicked the feeble beam on and off a couple of times to make sure it worked.

"All right," he said to Sylvia. "Do you want me to fight the lion?" Wiping away her tears with her fists, Sylvia grinned and clapped her hands.

23

My thoughts were not very nice as I followed Rochester up the stairs. I was so tempted to pick up one of the big nails that were lying on the steps and poke him in the rear with it—just so I could hear him scream. I shut my eyes and kept my jaw clenched just to keep myself from frightening Sylvia and Elaine.

"Ever find anything in these rooms up here?" he asked.

"No," I lied. I had found a ghost, but I wasn't about to tell him about it.

"If the house is going to be mine, I'll have to clean all of this out," he said in a very grown-up voice.

Rochester went first, I was second, and little Sylvia was right behind me. Elaine was pushing her up the stairs. We ran into a box that had been tipped over. Flowing out of the box was a fur stole with black fox feet dangling from it.

"Is this what scared her?" Rochester asked, picking up the fur and examining the silly looking feet.

Sylvia backed down into Elaine.

"It's just a little fox fur," Elaine said to her. It's not a real animal."

I guess Rochester was up to an adventure, for he was not stopping. One has to remember that he had been to the top of the stairs once before. But this time when he kept going, I was determined to go with him. This time we had a flashlight. I was going to follow him come hell or high water (I wasn't sure which would be worse). When he got going, he began to moan like a ghost. "Oooooooh," he said eerily to the stairs. Now I was convinced that the ghostly voice I had heard earlier had been his. However, I would wait to see what else happened before I revealed what I knew.

After reaching the top of the stairs, he turned to the right. I was hardly breathing as he approached the door to the room. In my mind I could still see the ghost waving at me as I scrambled away. I caught my breath when he turned the knob and pressed open the door. Right behind him, I peered under his arm as he focused the flashlight into the room. I trembled. The same ghost stood by the window, looking eerie in the fading light. It was waving at us! I couldn't help it. I let out a scream.

I screamed bloody murder. It even frightened me. Rochester jumped. Sky high. The flashlight leaped out of his hand and landed on a box of hats.

"Oh my heck!" Rochester said. "What was the bloody scream for?"

Little Sylvia fell backwards on the stairs behind us, and it was all Elaine could do to hold on to her and get her back up again. She began to cry.

"The ghost!" I shouted. "There's a ghost by the window. And it moved!"

"A ghost?" Rochester's face looked like a dishrag just wrung out of dishwater. "I don't see no ghost."

"There!" I shouted, pointing and feeling phlegm crowd my breath. "Can't you see! It's moving!"

"You're kidding me," Rochester said, picking the flashlight up out of the hats and shining it directly at the window. The light made everything different. Now I could see the small crack in the top of the window, I could see that the breeze was blowing the curtains, and that standing by the window was a tall . . . thing. Whatever it was, it looked like a ghost in a sheet, and I swear it was waving at us.

24

"That ain't no ghost," Rochester said. "When I opened the door, the breeze come through here," he said disdainfully, using bad grammar. "The breeze makes things move. There's a coat rack or something covered with a sheet."

No! I couldn't believe it. Now I watched the sheet waving at me and I withered inside. There was a perfect explanation for everything. I wanted to scream again, but this time it might have been at myself. For being so foolish.

"Rochester," I said in as stern a voice as I could. "Did you scare us when we were up here before?"

"Scare you?" he said. "You mean little ol' me? Become the green-eyed monster?" He turned around and put the flashlight under his chin. If you ever put a flashlight under your chin, you know what it does to your face. The light shines up through your jaw full of teeth and makes you look pretty much like a red skeleton. "Aaaaagh!" He twisted his other hand into the shape of a claw and tried to make like a ghoul. The "Aaaaagh" sounded a lot like the other frightening sound we'd heard.

I was empty of screams. Spent. I couldn't even get up a good "Oooooh." I just stood there looking into the dark room at the old ghost. I was still puzzled by the twists and turns of fate.

Elaine was backing down the stairs with Sylvia. Little Sylvia was still sobbing and Elaine was saying, "No, no. Don't be scared. It's just Rochester. He thinks he's the green-eyed monster."

"Well, can we see what's under the ghost?" I finally asked, hoping to stop this Halloween mishap in favor of a nice holiday devoted to angels and wreaths. "Let's take the sheet off. Just to make sure it's not a skeleton."

Rochester dropped the flashlight from under his chin, restored his claw to a normal-looking chubby hand, and turned to climb over the boxes in the room. He focused the flashlight on the tall "thing" in the ghostly white sheet, and I followed him cautiously through the obstacle course of trunks and old chairs until we reached the window. At first Elaine and Sylvia didn't follow us, until they decided we were serious. All of us stood in awe in front of the fake ghost, wondering what was before us.

It was Rochester who had the nerve to pull the sheet down. Holding the flashlight in one hand, he pulled on the sheet carefully at first, and when it slipped forward, he began to pull furiously.

It was the macaroni Christmas tree!

25

The room began whirling around my head, and I thought I was going to fall down. I felt I was the size of a cockroach watching everything tilt over me.

"We found the stupid tree! It's just a stupid cone of cardboard glued with macaroni," Rochester said. "Wasn't that what she wanted to put up in the living room because she's allergic to pine needles?"

Rochester handed me the flashlight, and very carefully slipped his arms under the round cardboard base of the tree. The girls were standing at my elbows oohing and awing. Sylvia was drying her tears with her chubby fist.

"If we're careful with this thing we can carry it downstairs," Rochester said.

"Wrap it back up in the sheet," I said. But Rochester had already cradled the base of the tree in his arms, and he began carrying it toward me. The girls and I backed through the door, and Rochester ducked down so far he was walking with bent knees only inches from the floor. I thought he was going to start crawling, but he got through the door into the hall landing admirably well, and sat on the seat of his pants on the stairs so that the tree could have all the room in the stairwell while he slipped and scooted down with it.

74

By the time Rochester finally got to the bottom of the stairs, leaving a long trail of flying macaroni as he still juggled the tree in his arms, Sylvia and Elaine had already run into Aunt Selby's bedroom to fetch Mom and Dad. But there was a crowd there, and nobody was coming out. In fact, there were jangling sounds of discord in Aunt Selby's sick room. I could hear Aunt Virginia's voice, high and piercing.

"I never went to court to contest it, because you always said you had the papers. And after all, I was in Colorado. But now there is no sense in you leaving the house to a shirt-tail nephew when we have a direct male heir."

I been clever enough to realize that the shirt-tail nephew was my father. Virginia would have moved heaven and earth to make sure that Rochester, and not my family, would inherit the house. When she heard we had moved in with Aunt Selby, she had gone berserk, even going so far as to bring her attorney, who was now the mayor, to draw up the necessary papers to get it into her hands.

When I approached the adults standing in the bedroom, I couldn't see anything through Chandler Stockton's blue-blazered back. But I could hear Aunt Selby wheezing and breathing with great difficulty. She was trying to talk.

"I do have the papers," she said in a small voice. "I do have the papers."

"Well, then, for goodness sake, get them out so we can see them, or I will have to go to court, Selby," Virginia said.

"I do," Selby said. "I don't need to sign any documents." She retreated into a cough that shook her chest so hard I thought she was going to die right then and there.

"Perhaps we'd better wait for a while," the mayor said.

It was my mother who saved the day. "It's snowing. Why don't you all have dinner here?" She tried to smooth over the rough spots while Virginia was fuming like the smoke stack on a paper factory. "We'll have more than just cookies," Mother continued, "I have a ham that can be cut and warmed in a jiffy, and scalloped potatoes. Please do stay."

The mayor said he had to go before the snow got too heavy. "If this doesn't resolve itself, I'm afraid we'll have to have a day or two in court," he glanced at Virginia. "But thanks anyway, for the invitation. Perhaps we can solve it another time."

Virginia made a fuss about how she wouldn't be able to get back to the hotel if Chandler and Evelyn had no car and the mayor left her. My father said he would take them all if they stayed for supper. So she agreed to that, and all of the adults began to leave Aunt Selby's dark-paneled bedroom. To get out of their way, all three of us girls backed up in the hallway, practically knocking Rochester to the floor with his arms under the macaroni Christmas tree.

"Where shall we put it?" Rochester demanded.

When Aunt Virginia saw the tree in Rochester's arms, it startled her. She stepped to the side and put her hand on her throat. "Oh my stars! The broken car and porch, the popsicle

76

sticks, and now the stupid macaroni Christmas tree! If it were any other time of year, I could stand it!" And she walked with the mayor to the door, waved at him, and stood at the window while he trudged through the snow to his big limousine.

26

"Well, I guess we should put the Christmas tree on the table by the front window," my mother said, trying hard to ignore Virginia's temper tantrum and the mayor's threat to take the rightful-heir situation to court. "I'll cut and warm the ham." She went into the kitchen.

Rochester carried the tree to the front window. There was a nice marble-topped table there with fluted legs. My father took the lamp off the table and Rochester set the macaroni tree on the doily that had been under the lamp. Every time he moved it even slightly, one or two pieces of macaroni flew off, clattering to the table or the floor. Soon people began stepping on it, making a noisy-crunchy sound as they walked around the table.

"See if you can bring Aunt Selby out to see it," I suggested.

Chandler and Evelyn were seated on the couch looking numb. It was as though they had never believed Aunt Selby would refuse to sign the papers. Especially when the mayor had come!

Daddy went into Aunt Selby's room and helped her get into her wheelchair. When he pushed her out into the room, she clapped her hands.

"Oh, it's wonderful!" Aunt Selby said. "I'm so glad you found the macaroni Christmas tree. Just in time for Christmas!"

Mother called me to help with the dinner at that point, so I'm not sure exactly what happened. But while I began peeling the potatoes I looked out of the kitchen toward the front hall, and I saw the mayor at the window of the door, knocking. He practically flattened his bulbous nose against the window when he put his hands up to look through. Virginia, who was right there almost immediately, swung open the door to let him in. He was covered with snow. It had come down that fast, in a dump. None of us were even aware of how much snow had come down. Snowflakes were lined up on his eyelashes and all over his hat, across the top of his shoulders, and in his lapel.

"I can't believe it," he said. "I can't even move the car back out of the drive."

The adults all looked at each other. Only two days until Christmas, and they might have to make up a bed for Mayor Crookston in one of the upstairs rooms.

I didn't like him much. And I resisted the idea. Elaine was jumping up and down, full of energy, as usual. Sylvia was sucking her thumb.

"Well, I'm glad you didn't get stuck somewhere in the middle of nowhere," Aunt Selby said. "Just take off your coat and relax."

The mayor sat down in a Queen Anne chair and bent over, looking glum. Virginia and Chandler and Evelyn gathered around him with their backs to everyone else in the room, as though they were trying to shut Aunt Selby out. At least that's what it looked like.

The dinner wasn't much better. Mother put big slices of ham on a platter. She asked me to open a can of pineapple, and to get on the stool and up to the spice cupboard to get down the cloves. I stuck cloves in the pineapple, and put the pan of ham into the oven. Mother helped me peel the potatoes, and we put cream of mushroom soup and cheese in the glass baking dish and put that in the oven on the rack under the ham. Mother had bought a couple of loaves of fresh bread at the bakery, and she asked me to put the chokecherry jam in the little glass dishes. Elaine helped to set the table. It looked very nice. I was thinking to myself: *Why are we making it so nice for Virginia and Evelyn, Chandler, and Rochester? And the mayor?* But I didn't say anything. I did everything Mother asked me to do.

27

"Dinner's ready," my mother said. "Come and sit at the table."

Virginia and Evelyn led the way while my father and Chandler tried to make some conversation with the mayor.

"Where did you go to law school?" my father asked, trying to show an interest.

"Valparaiso," the mayor said, as though he were simply giving the information by rote, as though his mind still sat in the automobile stuck in the snow. He wasn't about to look anybody in the eye and answer stupid questions.

"My father graduated from Valparaiso," Daddy said.

The mayor didn't answer him, but leaned forward in his chair and put his stubby hands on his knees as he got up. "Oh yes," he said, finally. "My, yes."

His answer didn't fit my dad's comment, but no one paid any attention. Virginia and Evelyn were whispering to one another while Chandler pushed Aunt Selby's wheelchair up to the table. Then he pulled out the chairs for the two ladies and sat them together on the east side of the dining room table. It was the first time any of them had been in their family dining room for many years. They made note of it. "My, Father's decor was always quite cavalier." It was as though they were smacking their lips. Virginia was eyeing the Grecian vases and grapes that danced along the border of wallpaper under the cornice. "Grandmother loved Keats. And she put that strip up in the dining room to remind her that every moment she must capture life—like the figures in Keats' urn."

Both the dining room and the living room were crowded with elegant furniture. Huge tasseled drapes on massive cornices hung at both the front and bay windows. Made of heavy brocaded silk, they shimmered like broken water. I noticed that the mayor was eyeing everything up and down also, his bald head glistening in the light from the chandelier. "My, yes," he was saying. "My, yes."

Mother had set the white cloth with her flowered china. Elaine had set each place with the gleaming silver. There were little salads we had fixed with canned tangerines and iceberg lettuce. Mother had sprinkled a little coconut on each salad, and a couple of slivered almonds. It looked very festive.

Once we were all seated around the large table, my father called on Chandler to say the prayer. Chandler had a booming voice and he gave a prayer that would certainly have reached heaven. But it would have been one of those prayers heaven had probably heard many times before. "Thank you for all of our blessings. Please bless this food to our good," Chandler intoned.

When he had finished, Mother asked me to help serve the food and I got up to get it. We brought the ham steaming on the platters, and took the scalloped potatoes from the oven.

Imagine my surprise when I carried the food in to the table, and heard Virginia say, "You haven't done anything to improve the house, Selby."

I cringed. I set the potatoes down on the cloth and ducked back into the kitchen for the rolls and the butter.

"It needs a lot of work that only a man can do around here," Chandler was saying.

When I set the butter down on the table cloth, I ducked into my chair. I wasn't even half prepared for what was about to occur.

28

It was a good thing there was food, because it made a safe topic for conversation.

"My, Frances," Virginia said, taking good-sized helpings. "What delicious rolls! How did you manage to do these scalloped potatoes? They're so creamy."

"This is so nice of you to have us here," the mayor said. "I hope I can bring Mabel next time."

"That would be lovely," Mother nodded.

"Perhaps the house will be transferred by that time," Virginia dared to say, bringing up the *dreaded subject*. I felt the words move over the candlelight like a knife. "And we can host you in a big Christmas Eve party."

If words were visible I would have seen a big sword pop out of Virginia's mouth and slide across the flames.

Aunt Selby sat up in her wheelchair like a bolt of lightening touched her. "I'm not dead yet," she said.

"Oh, Virginia didn't mean . . ." Evelyn was about to protest. But Chandler slapped her hand under the table.

"It's about time we discuss it, Selby. You are unable to care for the house. If we made a transfer now, before Christmas, we would save taxes."

Virginia's eyes narrowed. "You have forgotten about the will. Selby has the will, don't you, Selby?" The table was completely hushed. Not a fork rattled on a plate. "You know you have the will, and you know what it says. You've just been keeping it hidden from us because you don't want to face the fact that Papa, may his soul rest in peace, willed his property to his oldest daughter."

The words echoed in the old room as though Papa Bale were listening from behind a very thin veil.

No one said anything. My mother was blushing. My father looked down at his plate.

"I've lived here longer with Papa than anyone," Virginia said. "He would want me to give it to his only male heir, and that happens to be Rochester."

Everyone's eyes turned to Rochester. He seemed to be the only one eating. He had a string of celery hanging out of his teeth. His head was so close to the table his chin was practically in his plate. When he looked up the whites of his eyes were all we saw. He didn't say anything, but kept on crunching his celery.

Selby was usually pretty dignified. But something snapped in her now. "I don't blame you, Virginia, mind you. But when you left for Colorado you left me to take care of

Mama before she died. It was fourteen years. You came back from Colorado exactly once."

"I've heard that before. A thousand times. You always bring it up," growled Virginia. "You had a male heir so you always thought you would be the lucky recipient. But Beauregard died." The quiet was so penetrating, I could hear the mayor breathing. "Rochester is the rightful heir."

"Rochester?" Selby said. The fire was so hot between the sisters it was as though there were nothing else in the room. "He's only thirteen years old."

"Fourteen," Rochester said behind a mouthful of scalloped potatoes.

"Bill has just as much right to the house, if not more. You may be the first child, but his father Edward McKinsey was the first son."

We were hearing a litany of the family genealogy. But it looked like the family tree was about to break.

"No, we're not trying to . . . if you think . . ." my mother began.

But my father put a quick hand on her hands under the table. "We shouldn't quarrel about it," my father said. "If we have difficulties we should talk them out."

"What do you think I'm trying to do?" Virginia said. I thought Aunt Virginia looked like the Witch of the North.

"Let's be pleasant," Father said. "We're still family. Things are not as important as the family. We should get along with each other. After all is said and done, all we really have is each other."

"Well, I'd get along better if we could find that will," Virginia said.

"Well, I hope you don't look for it until I'm gone," Selby said, lowering her eyes and covering up a little cough with her old curled hand. "I don't need somebody roughin' up all my papers and going through my attic unless Billy wants to do it."

"Oh no," Mother said. "We don't want to . . ."

"It's most important we approach this with calm," Daddy said. "It's Christmas time. Can't we wait to talk about it after the holiday has passed? We'll solve the problem somehow."

"You hope by putting it off . . ." Virginia began. But Chandler put out his hand to quiet her while Mother got up from the table to get the second tray of rolls.

Rochester rolled up a piece of ham in his fingers and stuck it in his mouth. It looked like he was chewing on a big cigar.

29

There was a sullen moment of dead silence while Rochester chewed his piece of rolled-up ham. How he could chomp on the meat while everybody was watching him I can't guess, but he did it, looking up at everyone at the table with the whites of his eyes hanging out.

Then he did an amazing thing. He stuffed the entire meat roll into his mouth, put both hands on the table flanking his plate and half-stood out of his chair, leaning over with his napkin falling off his shirt. "What is everybody looking at me for? I didn't ask for the hulkin' house."

A draft came through the dining room as cold as though a ghost had slipped out of the kitchen and zipped through my father's hair. He averted his eyes from Rochester, but it wasn't a ghost he was looking for. It was my mother who had just walked through the dining room.

"If you liked the rolls, I'd be happy to give you the recipe." She was obviously trying to change the subject. She glared a terrified glare at Rochester, but asked no questions as to why he was half out of his chair. She must have heard what he said as she came in.

Virginia took the fattest roll off the top of the basket while Rochester sat down.

"Are you about ready for dessert?" my mother said. "It's a big surprise! Strawberry flambé. Have you ever seen strawberry flambé?"

"No, just McKinsey flambé," I heard Papa mutter under his breath.

I don't think anyone else heard it, or they were just too embarrassed to acknowledge it.

The strawberry flambé was a huge success. It came out of the kitchen in a cake pan with a little fire on the top of it, and strawberry jam spread on the sides like pink cellophane. Elaine clapped her hands and Sylvia began to sing out loud, "I am a child of God . . ." Her choice of subject matter gave us all a pause. No one had a moment's difficulty charging into his piece with a fork or spoon.

"We can have some Christmas music in the dining room," my mother announced when she stacked the plates and began to carry them out. "I know the mayor sings, and it's lucky Aunt Selby has a piano. Evelyn can play."

The mayor was smiling, putting his fork down from the last bite of flambé. He had practically dug the flowers off of his plate to get the last crumb. "Certainly," he said.

"Oh, will you sing *O Holy Night*?" Virginia said. "I love to hear you sing *O Holy Night*!"

"Of course," the mayor lowered his head demurely with a display of humility befitting a dignitary who had just witnessed an entire roll of ham disappear into the mouth of a fourteen-year-old boy.

"Can I dance?" Elaine tugged on Papa's sleeve. "Let me and Lindy dance. Can I dance to *Jingle Bells, Jingle Bells?*"

"Of course we can do *Jingle Bells,* and you can dance," Papa assured her, smiling.

For a few moments it looked as though the pre-Christmas dinner was going to survive. Even Virginia pulled away from the table and hobbled on her heels to the living room with a half-smile on her face. Unless it was just a post-flambé gas pain.

Aunt Selby found the music in the piano bench and gave it to Evelyn. Evelyn was a good pianist. You'd think she had rehearsed for a couple of hours. The introduction was flawless. And the mayor's voice was the biggest I had ever heard close up. He could sing with gusto, and all of us just sat transfixed listening to him. *Oh holy night, the stars are brightly shining. It is the night of our dear Savior's birth.*

The only thing better would have been if it were Christmas Eve. But that wouldn't be until the day after tomorrow. My dad had plugged in the lights on the macaroni Christmas tree, and lit the big wax Christmas candles in the ring of holly and ribbons on the piano.

Long lay the world, in sin and error pining, 'til he appeared and the soul felt its worth.

For a few moments we were family and friends together. We were thinking about Christmas. Perhaps we had forgotten the fight in the dining room.

But what happened next, after the song, had the direct result of throwing us all into a total state of panic. It was time for Elaine to dance, and, grinning from ear to ear, she was not going to let Papa go back on his promise.

30

"Does she need music?" Evelyn smiled helpfully, still at the piano bench.

"Oh goodie!" Elaine shouted, but before Evelyn could get her hands on the keys, my sister began to sing, "Dashing through the snow. On a one-horse open sleigh." And she began to fling her feet outward as though she had ants crawling somewhere in her clothes.

"Just a minute! Let me get started at the beginning," Evelyn said.

I must have been turning four or five shades of pink. My face felt hot. My sister was making a fool of herself, and she looked stupid without her shoes. Her socks began slipping off of her feet at every step.

Evelyn's request to start over did not daunt Elaine for a moment. She paused just long enough to make sure Mrs. Stockton was sitting ready at the piano keys.

"Dashing through the snow," she belted. At least this time Mrs. Stockton was with her.

It was the stupidest dance I ever saw, of course. She did not know how to dance and simply exploded with energy when she had an audience, no matter who it may be.

Everyone was trying to be polite. Mother and Dad were gripping each other's knees.

And then suddenly, not missing a beat, Elaine swooped her hand to the floor and pulled off a sock. Throwing her arms up, she tossed it in the air. It landed on the cornice of the front room drapery.

Grinning with celebratory glee, she swooped down again. Perhaps she had not realized the destination of her first wayward sock, for she swiped the second loose sock from her other foot and sent it also fluttering after the first. Both socks graced the sophisticated ivory-colored brocade cornice above the draperies, above the lighted macaroni Christmas tree, like migratory birds having found their holiday perch at last.

Though it daunted Elaine not at all, Evelyn paused in the music, and Mother stood up out of her chair. However, she had always been so careful not to crush any creative efforts of her child, that she forced herself to sit back down again. She gripped her hands together until her knuckles were white.

"Jingle bells, jingle bells," Elaine sang until I thought she'd never quit.

"That's good, dear," my mother clapped loudly.

It wasn't good, but I, too, believed it might have been the only way to end this ongoing disaster.

When she stopped playing, Mrs. Stockton looked up at the newly-decorated cornice above her. Two dirty gray-soled socks stared down at all of us like old cabbages.

"Oh, my goodness," my mother said, "It's quite a high ceiling. I don't know how we're going to get those down."

"I'll get them down!" The plot thickened. It was Rochester who rose to the occasion. Before any of the adults had gathered the gray matter of their brains to think of what to do, he had catapulted out of his chair and dragged it near the table that stood under the macaroni Christmas tree.

"It isn't hard to reach it from the chair," Rochester said, clumping all one hundred thirty pounds of him, or more, up on the chair, and stretching to reach the first sock. He plucked the sock off the top of the cornice like an apple off a tree. Proud of himself, he dangled it to Elaine, who ran to fetch it with a pre-emptive exclamation of gratitude.

"Oh, oh, oh!" she screamed.

Rochester glowed. But what happened next froze all of us who were seated in the room on the edges of our chairs.

When the cavalier Rochester began reaching for the second sock with a confident grin, he . . . can we say . . . *stretched* too far. Discharging a barbaric groan, he sailed over the macaroni Christmas tree, falling from his perch, smashing the cardboard and pasta tree into an explosion of macaroni and crushed paper to the living room floor.

31

Evelyn jumped off the piano bench so fast, she hit the keyboard, and the terrible sound of clashing notes accompanied Rochester's fall.

In a split second, there he was, lying in the middle of the living room floor like a tomato in a macaroni salad. The cardboard and paper had softened his descent. But some of the macaroni had disintegrated into powder and was catapulted vast distances like buckshot, flying in everyone's hair. Little pieces of macaroni landed in my father's eyebrows, and he looked surprised, like an Edmund Hilary who had just realized he still had a few miles to go before he reached the top of Mount Everest.

My mother ran into the kitchen to fetch the dust pan and the broom. Sylvia began to cry. And Elaine, who saw that one of her socks still hung on the cornice, was looking from Rochester to the chair to the sock, probably wondering if she she would have better success if she were to make an attempt to get it. Even Aunt Selby began parting her macaroni-laden hair away from her eyes.

"Oh, my stars!" Aunt Virginia gasped. She stood and backed out of the way as though she were looking at the destruction of Pearl Harbor. There were at least a dozen pieces of macaroni on her head, stuck in her curls.

Chandler rushed to Rochester. "Are you all right, son?"

"Oooh." Rochester was groaning. He didn't get up right away. Now he looked like both a tomato and a sausage stirred into all that macaroni—trying to pull himself loose, but finding himself stuck in it, like a casserole.

"Oh my stars!" Virginia repeated, for lack of something better to say.

Beneath Rochester's body, where the macaroni lay in hills and valleys, the paper cone of the macaroni Christmas tree revealed itself to be flimsy newsprint layers under a couple of poster boards so smashed they could barely be read. But when Chandler pulled them away from Rochester, we could see they were identical posters that said, *Corn Harvest Jig, Admission $1.00. Have the time of your life: Square Dance. Jig music by Ranch Hand Harmony, Bonneville Stake House, October 4, 1908.*

"Oooh," Rochester continued groaning in escalating scales of terrible pain as his father and mother tapped and pulled on his vulnerable limbs. "Does it hurt here?" "Does your back hurt?" "Should we move him, I wonder?"

Rochester swatted his father's hand away with a swift smack. "I can get up," he said in words almost unintelligible, like "Ikkingiddup."

When he rolled over in that mess, a surprising thing happened. Aunt Virginia gasped and knelt in the middle of that macaroni salad-like potpourri. "Oh, my stars!" she gasped, which is the unique statement she'd been repeating for several moments. "Oh my stars!"

Suddenly she had everyone's attention as Rochester raised himself. She let go of his elbow and knelt to the crushed paper and macaroni under him, scratching through it like a puppy dog looking for a bone.

"What is this?" She was ecstatic. "Oh, my stars!"

"What is what, Mother?" Chandler helped Rochester roll off the pile.

"Oh, my stars!" She had scraped away enough macaroni to fill a couple of garbage cans. A large light-colored paper began to show through. "It's a legal envelope."

"No!" Chandler looked at the light-colored envelope and became dog-like himself, scraping and scratching. It was a very interesting sight to see two dogs—mother and son—pawing away at the mess so fast that more macaroni flew. I envisioned one of them might lift up a leg like a doggy about to use a fence post.

While the paper and macaroni vaporized, Chandler began to breathe heavily. "It looks like the papers you were looking for, Mother," he said.

"Oh yes! It does!" Virginia cried out. She had a look on her face like a starved animal. "This is it! How long have you used this macaroni Christmas tree, Selby?"

Selby was dumbfounded. She sat watching the detritus of her macaroni Christmas tree flying in waves of pasta and dust all over the room.

"I'll bet it has been since 1908. Is that when you made this tree? After the Corn Harvest Jig, at the Bonneville Stake House with the Ranch Hand Band?"

But Chandler didn't wait for Selby to answer. He was so excited he grabbed the edge of the envelope from the floor and nearly ripped it open.

Virginia was still rambling on. "Selby, did you really forget these papers were here? Oh, my stars!"

"I don't think so. No, I don't remember." Selby looked as surprised as the rest of us.

As Chandler drew the papers out of the envelope, he rose to his feet, leaving Rochester still sitting in the mess and my mother beginning to clean it up.

"Come to the table, Chandler," Virginia said, tottering on his arm to get up.

They raced to the dining table which my mother had cleaned off only moments ago.

"Yes! These are the papers," Chandler said. "This is the will." He had pulled out the sheaf of papers and laid them out on the table. The rest of us gathered around.

32

"Oh, how appropriate!" Evelyn clasped her hands. "If these are the papers, this could be the greatest Christmas gift we have ever had."

All of us, including the mayor, got a chair around the table and leaned on our elbows, looking at the envelope. It said HOUSE FILE on it.

"Make no mistake about it," Virginia intoned. "These are the papers. I remember Father using these legal-sized manila envelopes when I was a girl." Anxiously, she reached out for the string around two little brown circles and began to untwist. But Chandler took over.

"All right," Chandler said. "Now we'll see just what your Father's wishes were. We must all agree to go by whatever he said." He stopped for a moment and glanced at Aunt Selby. "Selby, do you agree to go by whatever Grandpa Bale says?"

Aunt Selby looked as though she could be knocked over with a feather. She smiled faintly. I do think she was telling the truth when she said she hadn't known her father's papers had been locked up in the macaroni Christmas tree all this time. Or maybe she had forgotten she had put them there, and now that they had been discovered she could faintly recall that years ago as a crafty teen she had made and stuffed the macaroni tree. Or perhaps she had made the tree after the harvest dance and her father and mother thought it a good place to hide the house file.

However it had happened, it was now visible before us as we sat around the table holding our breath to see what was next.

When Chandler took the envelope out of his mother's hands, I thought, "How like mother, like son." Virginia was right there still drooling like the Hansel and Gretel witch.

I found a chair in the kitchen and dragged it through the den. However, I didn't sit for a minute, but stood at the window pushing aside the curtain to see how it looked outside. I couldn't believe what I saw. It was still snowing. The big flakes were coming down fast; it looked like another three inches had already fallen on the ground.

I wondered how the mayor would ever get his car out of the driveway. I looked at Virginia and Chandler and Evelyn and the mayor, and I imagined my mother trying to put them up in all the rooms.

When I brought the chair in to the table I couldn't find a place to put it until my mother, who had Sylvia on her lap and my dad, who had Elaine on his, made a little space for me between their chairs. We watched Daddy's cousin Chandler slip the papers out of the envelope. There were several packs clipped together with paper clips.

"Yep, these are the papers, all right," said Chandler, looking them over with his real-estate eyes."

All of us were still holding our breath. Chandler was scooting his finger along the lines. He thumbed through several other pages to find what he wanted to find.

"Well, what is it?" Virginia said. "Tell me, Chandler. I'm sweating like a hog."

You look like one, too, I wanted to say. But I didn't say it. I just looked silently at Aunt Virginia with the most disgusted look I could. I noticed that my mother looked straight ahead and not once changed the expression on her face.

Chandler wasn't quite able to make out what he wanted to see. He thumbed through a few more pages. "Hmmm," he said. "I'm not sure exactly what this means. Mayor Crookston, you're a lawyer. Can you figure this out?" Finally Chandler was admitting he had been stumped.

Virginia reached for it. She wanted to make heads or tails of it, but it was mostly tails. When she looked, she shook her head. "Says *library*. *Library*. He must have been drawing them up in the library."

Chandler shoved the papers over to the mayor, who reached into his handkerchief pocket and pulled out his glasses. As bald as a billiard ball, he looked like a duck when he perched the spectacles on his nose. "Well, all right, let's see what you have here," he said in an official tone of voice. He peered at the papers through the bottoms of his lenses. "Hmmm," he said. "I can't quite . . ." But then he put his finger on the lines that Chandler had read. "I . . . I'm just not sure, but I . . ." he continued reading. "Yes. Yes. All right. Oh, my . . ."

We waited while the mayor's bald head bobbed in the dining room light. "Why, I believe . . . yes! It's true."

He took off his glasses and his eyes darted around the table taking in the expressions of everyone who sat there.

"What's true? What's true?" Virginia cried.

"I'm sorry," the mayor said. "It's true. That is the case, which was very generous of your grandfather. This house is worth at least forty thousand dollars!"

"What's the case?" Virginia was almost screaming. "What's the case which was very generous of my father?"

The mayor cleared his throat. He seemed hesitant, as though he knew what he had to say would be unhappy news. "What a gift! You see right here," he said over a frog in his throat. "Your father wanted to donate . . ." He could barely get it out. "His house on the west side of town. Well, they had a library on the east side of town already. And he was so generous to think of the west side of town. To donate his home—this house—on the west side of town . . ."

Virginia breathed in and out as though she would jump across the table.

The mayor read outloud, ". . . to be used as a library for the young people on the west side of town, so they will have better access to books—at least as much access as the young people on the east side of town. And they can use my books as a beginning to their collection." He paused. "The city may have the house free, he says here. And the library is to be called the Bale McKinsey Library."

The mayor moved his finger along the text lines of the document, and then he raised his eyes.

You could have heard a pin drop anywhere around the table. It was so quiet I thought I could hear the snow fall.

33

There was a lot going on while the mayor sorted out the papers and smiled at everyone, including the crestfallen Virginia, although she was making a valiant stab at being gracious. She kept murmuring under her breath, "A city library, a city library."

"I have a meeting tomorrow morning with the council, our last meeting before we disperse for Christmas," the mayor said. He turned to Virginia, "Your father is a gracious, generous man, and a library named after him will be a monument to all of the McKinseys. It's a lovely gesture and we'll take care of it in a way that is beneficial to all."

Sylvia was still crying, and Mother was trying to calm her. "'House," little Sylvia was saying.

"The house is going to be a library. With wonderful books in it," Mother said. "Isn't that wonderful?"

My father was quiet. He hadn't expected anything to come his way, really. But the revelation had put a damper on the party.

Mayor Crookston said he had to go now, snow or no snow. He would dig himself out if he had to. Virginia, Chandler,

Evelyn, and Rochester were welcome to go with him at this time. Virginia said that was fine, they would.

"Please come back for Christmas Eve," Mother said to everyone. "We'll have another dinner and sing carols."

"Well, all right," Virginia said.

I pulled the curtain aside in the dining room window. It surprised me. The snow had stopped.

"Four inches," Mayor Crookston said. "I can probably dig myself out of the driveway."

"We'll shovel a path," my father said to be helpful. He went to the back door and pulled on his parka. I could hear the shovel banging and clanking in the back entrance.

During the next day while we waited for Christmas Eve, we cleaned up the macaroni and hung a few more strings of lights around the front hall. Selby helped us make a few more popsicle-stick trees, and she showed us how to pinch the ends of long licorice sticks together to make graduated sizes of circles. We piled the circles up, and voila! A licorice Christmas tree! We baked four or five dozen more Christmas cookies and frosted them with green, white and pink loops, then added red hots and silver sprinkles. They were beautiful.

Mother called Virginia on the telephone to make sure they were coming. Virginia asked her this time if the mayor's wife could just stop by. He wanted to bring her to see the new library.

"We'd love to have them come to eat," said Mother. "Tell them six o'clock."

Virginia didn't say whether she thought they could or not, but she would try.

Mother bought a twenty-three pound turkey and several cans of cranberry sauce. She had been saving dried bread in a drawer and pulled it all out to make dressing. She was preparing yams with brown sugar, white potatoes and gravy. She made an apple-cranberry jell-O salad and the dough for the rolls. We tried to help her as much as we could. For me that meant doing anything she asked of me—carrying food to Aunt Selby, cleaning the bathrooms. For Elaine that meant keeping Sylvia occupied. Sylvia got all of the pans out of the cupboard and began banging them with a spoon. Elaine carried all the pans out to the screened back porch and shut the back door.

Virginia, Chandler, Evelyn and Rochester arrived in the rented car Virginia had been using, because their car hadn't come out of the shop yet. When they trudged into the front hall, Chandler looked around and said, "You know, I'll be awfully proud if they use this house for a city library. I feel all right about it now."

They'd had a day or two to cool off and get used to the idea. Rochester thought it was a jolly plan, and said so. He loved books, and could imagine them spread all over the place. He didn't know what it meant to inherit a house, anyway. It had all been like a big game of cards, and he had just drawn an unexpected hand.

Evelyn and Virginia didn't say a word, except to say nice things about Mother's cooking, and how much they had looked forward to Christmas Eve.

It looked a lot like a Thanksgiving dinner, with turkey and dressing and the hot rolls again. Only the lights, and the licorice and popsicle-stick Christmas trees reminded us it was Christmas. Aunt Selby had a small nativity set carved out of olive wood which her son, Beauregard, had purchased when he had flown into Israel on a mission of some sort during World War II. It sat on the piano laced with cotton balls to look like snow. All the rooms were filled with the aroma of turkey and dressing with nuts, apples celery, herbs and hot bread, and it smelled like heaven.

"I'm making a toast to the new library," cousin Chandler raised his grape juice high after my dad had said the prayer. "May Aunt Selby last many more seasons until that library becomes a reality, and until every child on the west side of town can visit this illustrious McKinsey Library and leave with a precious book in his hand."

I thought that was a gallant toast. Everyone, even Rochester, dressed spiffily in a charcoal gray sportscoat, seemed to agree good-heartedly and accept the verdict. Aunt Virginia still looked a little shell-shocked. But she tried to smile, raising her glass about three inches lower than anyone else, as if she had fewer muscles or none in her arm.

"This is a great occasion, and we can be together every year," my father said.

Virginia looked doubtful. But we raised our cups and drank the juice as though we were making a real toast at a rotary club or presidential dinner.

The mayor's car drove up just after 7:00 when we were finished eating and Mother was about to serve the French silk pie. All of us looked out of the dining room window when the big limousine stopped and we heard the doors open and shut.

On the passenger side we could see a little woman with dyed-black hair and a tiny peaked hat with a sequin-scattered veil. She was small, and her large fox collar seemed to swallow her completely. As the mayor opened her door and she got out of the car, we could see tiny leather boots with high heels and tops that came to her knees. Not seeming to mind the four inches of snow, she walked with mincing steps over to the front porch.

The mayor apologized profusely. It wasn't for dinner, he had come, he said. It was to show his wife Mabel the new library, and it would take only a few minutes. They had a family get-together of their own.

Mother pleaded with them to have some pie. She had plenty and was hoping they would come.

Finally, the mayor said yes, thank you, they'd have some pie. He stood in the foyer with Mabel and pointed out the open staircase, the banisters, the skylight at the top that illuminated the stairway, the wide wood floors, the carpet, the ivory brocade drapes, and the stunning cornice.

"As you can see," he said to Mabel, "the dining room is beautifully paneled with oak wood and Chinese silk. This raw silk must have been imported long before the beginning of the war."

Mabel smiled quaintly. Mother should never have given her a piece of pie. She took one bite and left the rest on her plate. Of course she ate like a bird because she looked like a bird.

Everyone was glad to see the mayor and Mabel. They smiled. They were kind. We sang Christmas carols. The mayor insisted on taking Mabel up for a look at all the rooms, the bathroom, my folks' bedroom, the rooms where Elaine and I and Sylvia slept. They poked around Aunt Selby's room. Aunt Selby was very quiet through all of the festivities. I think she was wondering if it was up to her now to just die.

All was very peaceful and lovely until we finally began the program. There were no socks floating upwards, no smashed Christmas tree. When it was finally time for the mayor to sing, that was when the last strange thing happened on Christmas Eve. We overheard Mabel say sweetly to her husband, the mayor, "It will do. Yes, it will do nicely."

The mayor blushed only a moment. "Yes, well," he said to my mother. "The Provo City Council said they can handle the expense of only one large library, so they won't have to acquire duplicate collections. They will use the house for something else. Perhaps as a residence for a special city official. They appreciated Bale McKinsey and his donation and have great respect for his generosity."

It is to my mother's credit that she never blinked an eye. "We still hope you will sing to us, Mayor Crookston. This is Christmas Eve and you and your lovely wife are far from home."

I thought, *No, Mother, they are at home.*

The mayor's voice sounded even more beautiful than before, if that was possible. He sang *O Holy Night* by request, and *Oh Little Town of Bethlehem* and *The First Noel.*

Finally, he graciously took Selby's hand and held it for a long time. "The house is yours, my lovely and gracious lady, for as long as you want it. This is the greatest Christmas gift ever given to our grateful city. We shall always remember you and your father for his love for books, and for his generosity and kindness—a gift of Christmas."

Christmas was a magic time, a blessed, glorious time of Christ's birth. No one would appear to be so selfish or materialistic as not to obey Grandfather Bale's wishes.

My mother held all of us girls in her arms, when Elaine said, "We can't live in the house?"

"No. A house is a place, a thing," Mother whispered. People quarrel over things. We have each other, and that is more precious than a house. We could live in a little place and be happy. Not because of the walls around us, but because we are together, and we share love."

All of us sang *Silent Night.* And when we looked out the window, the white snow, like moth's wings, whirled around the lamplight and feathered down out of the sky.

AFTERWORD

Provo citizens may wonder why there was never a second library on the west side of town. Well, the macaroni tree, the popsicle sticks, and the McKinsey family may be mostly fictional, (although the family was drawn from the author's own experiences in Denver, Colorado), but it is a fact that a mansion on Fifth West was graciously donated for a library. And when the city could not afford to support such an endeavor, the mayor bought it as his personal residence, purchasing it from the city for $5,000.

The house still stands to this day, one of the most beautiful mansions in Provo.

Cedar Fort, Incorporated
Order Form

Name:_____

Address: _____

City: _____ State: _____ Zip: _____

Phone: (   ) _____ Daytime phone: (   ) _____

The Macaroni Christmas Tree

Quantity: _____ @ $10.95 each: _____

plus $3.49 shipping & handling for the first book: _____

(add 99¢ shipping for each additional book)

Utah residents add 6.25% for state sales tax: _____

TOTAL: _____

Bulk purchasing, shipping and handling quotes available upon request.

Please make check or money order payable to:
Cedar Fort, Incorporated.

Mail this form and payment to:
Cedar Fort, Inc.
925 North Main St.
Springville, UT 84663

You can also order on our website **www.cedarfort.com**
or e-mail us at sales@cedarfort.com or call 1-800-SKYBOOK